Praise for *Virgins In Rev*

"With this exquisitely twisted account of a psychic and alcoholic descent, Gabriel Hart transposes a Lovecraftian sensibility into the lower depths of contemporary Los Angeles. A murderous bender of a novel from a true original."

– **John Tottenham**, author of The Inertia Variations,
ANTIEPITHALAMIA & Other Poems of Regret and Resentment

"I have been told I am crazy all of my life. Not for a second has it made me doubt myself. I have been forced to accept it."
Caleb, Hart's insightful alcoholic protagonist, allows himself this confession to a psychologist – who is also defiantly manic – in a conversation that one could only call a 'breakthrough' by wondering how many laws and ethical codes can be broken by both parties in a single evening? But through the haze of blood and whiskey, the theory of blackout-as-possession begins to take weight as the reader considers the psychic geography of Los Angeles; its past, present and future, the spaces once inhabited and abandoned. The dead walk among us, and perhaps it takes the dissolution of the medial temporal lobes with alcohol to see that clearly. Most of us wouldn't wish that path on our worst enemies; Caleb's journey is a desperate one with no clear resolution, but one can't stop from following headlong into that psychological abyss with every word.

– **Dr. Rachael Polokoff, PhD**

VIRGINS
IN
REVERSE
&
THE
INTRUSION

A TRAVELING SHOES PRESS BOOK

VIRGINS IN REVERSE & THE INTRUSION

TWIN NOVELLAS BY

GABRIEL HART

TRAVELING SHOES PRESS
PO BOX 332
Pioneertown, CA 92268

Virgins In Reverse & The Intrusion
ISBN# 978-1-732-92051-4

First Edition | 2019
Edited by Jean-Paul L. Garnier
Book design by Jon Christopher

For C.B.
and
Puppet City

CONTENTS

Foreword by Tav Falco
11

VIRGINS IN REVERSE
13

THE INTRUSION
103

FOREWORD

E ntering the realms of Magic, Aleister Crowley warned, *innocence is no protection.* Enter then these two books, at your own risk.

Though tawdry, the cast of characters is utterly convincing because each unfolding word is lived and breathed by its author. No stories such as these can be phantasized – even imagined by mortal man. The central figure is Caleb, whose name in Hebrew denotes dog, but in his case it is the twin headed hound of Hades known as Cerberus.

Cecilia (See seal ya. She'll seal you off in your own private hell) is the voluptuous avatar of Aphrodite at whose feet Caleb worships in their temple of toil at the stigmatized Silent Movie Theater on Fairfax Ave. Her creamy cheeks wrap blissfully around the turgid, aching cock of Caleb, transforming the lonely London Fog trench-coated night crawler into her pet deep throat sex slave.

Then there's Amber, the lingering ex of Caleb – a tired gothic flophouse chic who nearly claws his arms off. While Amber is often regarded as a gemstone, it's not actually what you can call a stone. That's because Amber is a fossilized resin from ancient evergreen trees. This stone often exhibits little insects trapped inside while it was forming as a tree resin.

What becomes of this man guzzling a barrel of Rusty Nails in conference with his psychiatrist who has freshly fucked Cecilia on the same couch? Every known substance and folly are tried: dope, sex, brutality, but the time he was a teenager, alcohol was and has remained the constant vehicle, thrusting consciousness off the scale of any known standard of measurement; where memory, imagination, and gestalt pattern-recognition collide in a monstrous gavotte of self-abnegation.

Caleb is drawn to the darkest angular corners of tombstone underground Los Angeles: to bars where drinking is a ritualistic psychic splintering of mind from body, to inebriated love trysts among the bushes and detritus under an overpass of 101 freeway. Caleb holds the seeing hand with its glistening eye up to the mirror of moral rectitude and shatters it, exploding and shooting splinters and shards of glass off ninety miles an hour in all directions.

Fists in the face, emetic orgiastic frenzies of exhibitionist grandeur disorder the senses and lower thought processes until consciousness recoils to a pinpoint of sublime negation. "My mind momentarily wandered the gamut of irrevocable remorse, a silent eruption quickly extinguished by a catatonic haze, where thoughts go to die." Out of these pits of ashes rise the L.A. future-deathbilly, shock-cow roak form of Caleb as he morphs from psycho dwarf into a Bataillesque savant blown over again and again by ill winds larger, more fierce and more omnipotent than FATE itself.

It is said that insects will inherit the world, but in *Virgins in Reverse* & *The Intrusion*, they already have, and their mating and habits of procreation are widely emulated among the pages of both books. Beware reading these twin novels evoked from the dregs of Nathanial West. Funnier than Nelson Algren down and out with his harlots in New Orleans, more terrifying than psychedelic saints raising the undead. With outstretched arms, real zombies stalk these pages where the sun don't shine.

- Tav Falco, Vienna 2018

VIRGINS
IN
REVERSE

ONE

N ow. I would be cheating us if I were to ignore my first instinct for a more lucrative one. To chisel these words into a fairy tale that might bring great joy, hope, and a warm fireplace comfort to those who read it. However, I cannot and will not shield my face from the avalanche of reason that would immediately oppose this – most importantly, the fact that I simply know too much and often despise myself for it.

She and I met in a movie theater where a murder occurred but something was born there as well. Simmering through a two-year incubation period, it cut its teeth on being one of the most precious, egg-shell walking, all-knowing, dark end of the mind, telepathic affairs the city ever hushingly witnessed. We took care of it with our eyes and seldom spoke, as too many words would confuse or *cheat* something like this, something beyond us.

Not only was it an actual functioning silent movie theater - it was also the last of its kind. Unwavering since the silent era, still standing in defiance of all the obnoxious *progress* Los Angeles is known for, rendering everything transient. But the heart of one of the city's most obsolete institutions remained beating to everyone's perpetual surprise. We all know how it is here – if it hasn't been bulldozed, it's only because it has been pre-destined to become its own tombstone.

First greeted outside by framed portraits of Keaton, Lloyd and Chaplin, one would then walk through those creaking double doors, past the yellowed hand-painted posters and into the lobby, where a nostalgic dizziness would overtake you. Beyond eyes still adjusting to the dim lighting on its faded sunflower and crimson décor, it was a lightheadedness, perhaps a slight hesitation, known to strike those who tread into curious chambers where the clock has long stopped. The air itself still held the residue of some sordid molasses past. Even with all its grand invitation, offering the chance to time-travel by passing through a single threshold, one would often have the feeling of trespass – that perhaps their jaded presence could eventually chip away at the spellbinding atmosphere of innocence.

Innocence! *Innocence?* It didn't matter how many senile geezers from the neighboring convalescent homes would flock there every Sunday to fork over the small fee, only to vicariously live through these flipping images, reminding them of the simpler life. *Nothing* could ever erase the gory last act the theater hosted for its previous proprietor, Lawrence Austin. He was the golden child apprentice turned heir apparent to the theater's original 1930s owners, John and Dorothy, who re-opened the theater in 1991 after convincing a recently widowed Dorothy that the show must go on. This second phase was met with enough enthusiasm to keep it humbly running for six more years, with Larry, stylish yet with high mileage, taking the role as the creekily gay master of ceremonies. His balding hairline ingeniously whipped up from the sides into a coif like a soft serve ice cream, as he would give his delicately deadpan synopsis in front of the stage's trademark gold lamé curtain.

Now, when you choose not just your projectionist, but your lover as well, to be a man named James Van Sickle, any morbid foresight should come as no surprise and require little explanation – anyone that heard that name couldn't help but exclaim what a supremely cinematic name for a villain! Sneak-scrawling his name onto Larry's sizeable will after months of lover's turbulence, Sickle sealed the deal by hiring an impressionable Chicano gangster kid - traditionally naïve of consequence - to snuff out his lover. During business hours, no less. As a crowded theater watched the iconic silent film "Sunrise," Sickle conveniently sequestered himself in the boiling projection booth, sweating profusely with nothing but a small window separating himself from the scene unfolding… the young Cholo marching behind the concession stand where Larry miserly counted money with a teenage employee. As instructed, he shot Larry point blank in the temple, and for good measure, opened fire at the shocked witness in her chest. Quickly advancing into the darkened throng of the unsuspecting theater, he shot a couple times into the air for drama and confusion's sake, before retreating out the emergency exit. Larry died. The witness lived. Sickle and his henchman were caught shortly thereafter and the theater closed its doors once again, due to death of its owner. Most people in L.A. already know this story, long since dunked into the city's anecdotal reservoir for anyone to sip from and freely add their backwash regardless of whether or not they were actually there or bothered to fact-check their sources.

Fast-forward two years. We see failed forty-year old singer-songwriter trust fund brat in the midst of mid-life crisis – a Mr. Charles Lusterlatke. The man-child and his enabling Mother walked down Fairfax towards an early afternoon lunch at Eata-Pita. They pass the boarded-up art deco theater and its still dangling "For Sale" sign.

"Mommy, will you buy that for me?"

And with all the frustrated surrender of a housewife at the checkout stand, too tired to argue when her crying boy who wants jellybeans, she looked at him, looked at the theater, looked at the ground, then back at the theater, then began dialing the number.

TWO

"The Emerald Wasp (Ampulex compressa) is also known as the jewel wasp, due to the brilliant turquoise translucence of its exo-skeleton. It is the solitary specimen of the Ampulicidae family, but due to its distinction of unusual reproductive behavior, which in-volves stinging a cockroach and using it as a host for its larvae, it belongs to the larger group of entomophagus parasites..."

F acing out of the box office was a help-wanted sign that boldly demanded my attention as I was leaving the Silent Theater one brisk December evening, interrupting a one-sided conversation from my disappointing date. A girl named Amber, my *fluctuating* girl-friend who I rarely referred to as such. She was a Goth-damaged teeth-gnasher for whom I had nothing but a lonely coward's grip for at this point. When misery required company.

I rubbernecked the sign, slowing our pace. I faintly heard her complaining how cold it was, but I had already gone deaf, decision cemented. I walked back to the theater and asked for an application. While this was no more than a retread of five or so feet, the ab-surdity of me re-living my youth of working a string of dead-end theater jobs was something I had no business flirting with. A de-evolution. But sometimes you just see something – perhaps the tim-ing or the lighting is just right – that ends up resonating so deeply, no ambiguous rationale could possibly derail it. The decision has been made only from the mere sight of it, as future's history unfolds before our very eyes. No sense. No effort. It had been seen, and I forgot about Amber, again.

Within a week Mr. Lusterlatke called me in for an interview, telling me to wear "something nice, slacks, button-up, whatever, I just can't have you looking a bum". I raced down there looking roughly twenty bucks. A thinly veiled illusion were the dregs of my nice clothes - like putting perfume on a rotten egg, accentuating my blemishes and screaming all my day late insecurities – as a man will still reek of alcohol under brand new clothes. Reluctantly, I was hired – not after a proper interview, but rather being forced victim to an extensive tour around Charlie's inflated ego – the places he'd been, the people he knows, and how lucky I should consider myself to be employed by him. His tone of every word dripped with a high-flying over-confidence or disdainful, unfounded paranoia and not a damn mood in between, giving me blatant previews into the run-away tyranny he would soon be unleashing into our foundation, just as soon as I felt at home there.

The following afternoon I showed up for my first shift. After finding a parking space for my grey '88 Toyota Pickup, I gave myself one last look in the dim glare of my side window before walking to-wards the front door of the theater. It looked unnervingly deserted. I peered into the box office window only to see the curtains drawn and my reflection looking back, sheltering its blackened, transparent eyes with my curled hands. I approached the door and knocked – hesitating at first – but quickly graduating into a frustrated rap, as I began to think perhaps I had the wrong day or time. I pushed on the door and it swung right open, causing me to fall with it. It was my oldest reoccurring theme – to be made a fool by merely attempting to show some manners.

In the stale air of the lobby I looked both ways. Still. Not a soul. My ears perked up to frantic voices fading down from the upstairs, quickly followed by a soon to be all-too familiar sound – the invasive trample of Lusterlatke's shitty loafers skipping down thinly carpeted stairs, like a spoiled brat on Christmas who already knows that he is getting exactly what he wants. He descended to the lobby with a hop over the last three stairs, wearing one of his newly franchised "Silent Movie Theater" t-shirts tucked into black and white hounds tooth trousers with the most condescending newsie cap to match. This was the man's uniform, his own skewed image of antiquity colliding with a capitalist's keen eye for re-appropriation.

"Uh, yeah… can I HELP you?" he asked suspiciously, not trying to hide his callous who-are-you-and-what-the-fuck-are-you-doing-here sentiment.

"Yeah… I uh, work here? I was here the other day, remem…"

"Ah yes, yes, of course…" His eyes darted to and fro searching for any excuse for his oversight, "Come, let me show you around… I've already put the others to work."

My eyes followed his hyperactive light-foot trot down the side aisles into the darkness of the theater. I was dizzy, disoriented from the lack of light as Lusterlatke threw open the door to the patio, momentarily blinding me. I followed him out, stepping outside onto the terracotta to find two of my co-workers on their hands and knees, scrubbing the porous grout in between. They both looked up and waved, giving me similar half-smiles, eclipsed by a weariness that they failed to hide. Lusterlatke tried introducing them but I wasn't listening, as I had noticed a bright crimson-lidded head pop up from behind the bar and then quickly duck down again. My heart jumped, rattling my ribcage before falling to the pit of my aching stomach. The second I acknowledged the profound pain of this nerve-pulling displacement, she rose up again and began walking towards him, in an off-shoulder turquoise dress that seemed to boomerang the sun under a netted shawl, evoking a captured mermaid. I saw her wide eyes go sideways above her lip-biting smile, as she quickly disappeared into the darkness of the theater. As if I needed to be told to follow this walking flash of radiance, Lusterlatke motioned me into the theater.

Lusterlatke power-walked ahead of me, passing her, leaving the two of us walking down the aisle momentarily alone in the half-black. I saw her silhouette superimposed against the threshold of the lobby ahead. It was without a doubt the single-most revelatory figure of a woman I had ever seen – a sentimental teardrop with legs and a cherry on top. As she walked the light of the lobby beamed down on the rest of her, hitting first her fox-red head then quickly cascading to her shoulders and back, and where it should have merely dripped onto any lesser specimen, it exploded at her waist to reveal the bulging, arching contours of the single-most proudest ass I have ever fallen witness to. Religious in its permanence while almost architecturally obscene, I zeroed in on its jazzy, juggernaut pattern of movement. Like the silencing glory of two planets quaking before colliding, retreating, then forcing them back into each successive crash that would follow; this was not an act of destruction but merely a confident, cooperative effort on the part of her cheeks to prove to the world that they truly existed.

Whole moments passed before I realized that I was following her instead of our boss. It was clear I had chosen a different path – a different technique altogether – of his initial training. My blood had rushed to all of my outer limits, just short of purging through pores. It was so consuming that I even felt a regretful relief to see her disappear into her post at the confessional shroud of the box office. I went to my own station behind the concession counter as she double-backed out the other way from a blurred side view out of my eye. All I could do was sigh and imagine myself invisible, humbled by this private outburst.

The full cast of my co-workers suddenly converged in the lobby and surrounded me in half circle as if they were about to jump me in. Instead I got a rapid collage of questions and hospitable smiles.

"Hey look! A new guy!" the tall one said with an antiquated enthusiasm, "I'm the projectionist, name's Jimmy. What's yours?"

"Caleb. Nice to meet you all."

"That's a interesting name. Jewish? What does it mean?" someone else chimed.

"Uh, no. I mean, in a way... My lineage is half-Irish, half-English, but I denounce the English part cause I believe it's a lot like being a Jewish Nazi. The Brits enslaved the Irish, you know? What does it mean? Uh... I've heard it means either 'Dog' or 'Heart' but it seems like even the etymology scholars can't agree which..."

"He talks like a surf punk that's read too many books..." I heard someone whisper giggle.

"Yeah, well don't lose sleep over it." I said, deadpan. "Any bullshit eloquence left in me usually takes a nose dive after my fifth drink of the night."

"Well," said Jimmy, pointing straight at me, "sounds like we got a plan after work? We all usually feel pretty chewed up and go down the street for a few. Let's see ya get all primitive..."

"Okay, okay gather around. NONE of this leaves this table though..."

We were all at the Kibbitz Room down the street from the theater. The self-loathing but jovial Jimmy was holding court, initiating the rest of the group into the dense drama of the murder at the theater two years back. Jimmy had been in the projection booth at the time of the mid-afternoon snuff, but previous to the crime he would inherit a keen fly-on-the-wall perspective into the twisted relationship of Larry and Van Sickle. There we all sat, faces close, half-drunk, fists in our chins, excited to be privy to these secret histories.

Occasionally we looked both ways to make sure no one besides us was listening. The inherent paranoia wholly contagious as if we were suddenly accomplices.

"So. A *whole other* thing!" he half-whispered as he waved both arms, "There was this classic Fairfax Blvd. nut-job that used to hang right there in front of the theater every single day, just screaming his guts out at those portraits of Chaplin and Loyd as if they were real people that had done him wrong. The place was like his delusional shrine to what he believed to be the very cause of his shattered life! *Aaanyway*, Van Sickle hated this man and would lose his shit every-day going out there hollering sadistic obscene shit right back at him, as if the guy was his actual mental opponent. I mean, most of us learned to just deal with it like any other passing loon on this street but Van Sickle was like the Son of Sam and this guy was the barking dog, right? Obviously, this went on for far too long, the guy not missing his screamin' beat for anything, rain, nothing! Well, one day he was gone. Sure, transients come and go, but all the same we thought it was pretty out of blue. We asked Van Sickle what happened and all he said, very stern, was 'I took care of it and that's all you need to know.'"

We laughed, some nervously, some with suspicious head shaking.

"Chsssssssss…"

"Yeah, I know, I know… He could have been bluffing us to think that, some tough guy shit or whatever, but the big reveal is that when we came to work that day, he had a group of guys out there in back pouring cement over what was supposed to be part of the fucking garden, deciding that this would be a great place to put a couple trashcans, even though we already had them in the car port, out of the way and everything… So you guys are more than free to do the math yourselves, knowing he had Larry snuffed out there anyway…"

The six of us sat there squirming, gushing with scary, clairvoyant cackles. My attention went immediately to Cecilia as she threw her head back, mouth agape, staring wildly at the ceiling fan above us, tossing her cherry hair around a bit while her eyes just kept rolling right back into her head. I was possessed by a thought - vowing to distill that moment into a medicinal tincture so precious it was only to be used in emergencies, and until then, I would drink as much beer as time would allow in order to simultaneously suppress and unleash a poor man's placebo effect. Luckily, for perhaps less profound reasons, the rest of the table had the same idea, as there was soon no more room for our elbows, the clanking of empty glass taking up every spare inch of wood grain.

The evening ended as they would for many nights to come, stumbling back to the theater way past midnight to sneak in and have clandestine screenings for our new insular secret society; raiding the vinegar-reeking vaults to watch everything from 1920s monkey exploitation to bizarre fetish reels, throwing back flasks as our faces bathed in the warm sepia glow of ancient celluloid. I always made sure to sit close enough to her to swipe a glance whenever darkness would shield me - disciplined and sparing at first – until I began the audacious ritual of wearing my *Roy Orbisons* inside.

Even after these marathon midnight screenings no one wanted to stray from the flock. She would zero in, engaging me as if we were walking on a frozen lake of uncertain perils but in a way removed from guilt or real danger; and when I had to respond to something she said - it was a muted mumble as I would look down or to the side – anywhere but her target eyes, and like a bully she offered no apologies as she looked me dead on. Had she inherited all the confidence in the world? Was she downright hoarding it? Rarely did she pass without shooting a deliberate look. I would always look away until she had just about passed by, enough for me to see her looking straight ahead, satisfied, doing that same lip-biting smirk she had the first moment I saw her. To make matters more nerve-grating, when she initiated conversation, her eyes would first light up, followed by a huge smile and usually something ceremonial with her hands – a clap or a crossing, occasionally in a praying gesture – as if she had some big announcement or epiphany to let me in on. Even her most mundane declarations were wrapped in an air of sacred sincerity, and I would receive them just as diligently as if they were words from a genuine prophetess.

One day she made an announcement to the group, that her and the new bumpkin on the block we all referred to as "John Boy" were an item and were soon moving in together. I felt it right in my solar plexus, then moving worse into my confounding rationale. John Boy was a sweet enough kid to work with, but he was square as they come. Jimmy called him Howdy Doody, then "Boy Howdy" – as he looked and acted like a cross between Little House On The Prairie and that freckle-faced puppet himself. An Amish clown, the kid was! He was so unthreatening it actually offended me beyond that fact he just inherited my angel.

The modish horn-rimmed ticket-shredder named Merel was our reliable gossip hound. She instinctively shed some light on this for me, unsolicited. "She just got out of a long bad relationship and she told me she was trying to find the most painfully normal – even boring – guy she could find, just to coast for a bit, you know? I mean, the guy plays with model trains and collects bugs, no joke…

So, I guess she scored?" Her eyes were askew as her voice dissolved downward, sounding just as confused as I was. She abruptly walked away in errant strides, almost to drip dry from the condensation of my cold sweat.

It was a punishing brand of hand-shackled voyeurism that was to follow. No end in sight. I couldn't even throw my hands up to God to curse his name or else everyone would know my truly pathetic shoes! But I was a vet of doling out much harsher punishment to myself. The survival instincts came quickly, as I dismissed her as simply *out of my league,* remaining convinced of this for the next two years.

THREE

"Cockroaches are often found in dark, warm and moist areas inside houses, hotels and restaurants. Some species also thrive in sewers or outdoors. Most cockroaches hide in dark, secluded areas by day. They can be found behind furniture and appliances, as well as under refrigerators and stoves, in cupboards or cabinets. They are capable of flattening themselves in order to fit into crevices between floorboards and walls. Roaches are most active at night, during which time they forage for food and mate..."

My apartment at 5831 Harold Way was once accurately described as "the saddest place I have ever seen" by someone who barely knew me. I had landed there after a homeless summer, sleeping in my truck and squatting in a vacant old folks home in the Valley that smelled of old bedpans and gravy. Even with a solid roof over my head I never quite shook the destitution.

It was always dark inside. No matter how hard the sun tried to intrude it remained veiled behind the red plaid sheet I nailed over the window. This was essential to entertain the denial of my own filth, shrouding all the bottles, cans, bitten off corners of condom wrappers, records, and half eaten take-out in enveloping, deceptive shadows.

Upon entering, immediately to the right, you'd notice the browned blood smeared in frantic handprints covering a large area of the mirrored-door closet. The rest of this single room apartment was a product of pure neglect, the blood left up as a deliberate trophy. You see, in the middle of one particularly fierce three-day bender with Jack, my city beat brother-in-arms, we had morphed into a trio, acquiring a large black dude with guitar in tow, simply called "Bluesman." He would break into impromptu twelve-bar outbursts every time Jack or I would mention something he thought as song worthy, apparently everything out of our fucking mouths. As much of a pest as The Bluesman was, he was charming or maybe just convincing enough for us to let him stick around, sharing bottles upon bottles of Mad Dog 20/20. I even allowed him to crash at my place for one of those blurry, jagged nights. His presence would have been annoying, if not for the frequent reprieves where he would duck around the corner with whomever would eagerly approach him with a smile and a whisper, after which he would emerge counting a fistful of cash.

The tail end of the third night of bloodshot-eye alley-hopping and itinerant drinking saw the three of us upstairs at my neighbor Shelly's place, who was having a party we were not exactly invited to. The guests were predominantly Huntington Beach surf-Nazis – a breed I had spent half my life avoiding. The minute we walked in – first me, Jack, then The Bluesman caboose, a hush blew through the crowd followed by cowardly whispered racial slurs and muted laughter.

"Nigger... Nigger... Ha! Nigger!"

I, who by this time, had become quite attached to our new friend, lost my marbles and went straight to the biggest offender, throwing silver-tongued daggers until we were face to face in a war of petty insults. Jack noticed the gang gathering like a storm cloud and realized just how outnumbered we were. He hoisted me over his shoulders and carried me off, running down the stairs towards my apartment, followed by what sounded like an army of Gestapo boots. I fell off his shoulders when we got to my door and looked back to see seven of them running right toward us as I struggled to open the door.

"Get in! Shut the door! Lock the fucking door!" Jack screamed at me.

We hassled with the keys as they gained ground, almost in the door when they surrounded us like hungry zombies trying to penetrate my abode. I seemed to virtually flatten my body to get through. It swung shut as fast as it opened. Jack slammed the door on one of the intruder's arms, and as he raised it for another harder, hopefully crippling blow, the guy swung the door wide open. The whole battalion ran inside my room and a tornado of fists commenced. One blow to my face had already closed one of my eyes as I blindly *wind milled* through the maelstrom, until I witnessed Jack grabbing a guy by the head, forcing his cranium back and forth from the plaster into the mirror, against each opposing wall like a blood-soaked metronome. The rest of the gang lost their nerve at the sight of this one-man-army *Jackson Pollocking* their fearless leader's face onto the canvas of my walls, his struggling hands looking for a surface to grip ended up finger-painting in his own bodily fluid. And just like that, through the longest minute I have ever endured, they were gone.

I woke up the next afternoon with my head the last thing to leave my bed; the trauma of foreign fists adding what felt like an extra twenty pounds to an already throbbing alcoholic anvil of a brain. With that many participants every blow is a shot in the dark, but aside from Jack's main prey, I clearly came in second place. Further affirmed once I stumbled to the bathroom mirror, I saw the telltale trinity of a classic black eye with blood swirling into retina, swollen lip, and something black and blue that looked like it could give birth out of my forehead at any moment. A profound pang of defeat washed over me in a pendulous grip when I heard Jack's voice cut through the stale air.

"Hey, lookin at yerself is gonna do you no good! Come check out what we did to that guy in your hallway!" he chuckled, charitably.

That was somehow all it took to get a giggle out of me and slowly bring me out of my amnesia. I walked slowly to the mirrored hallway and rotated to the left to observe my reflection, only this time it was obscured by a wildfire of gore from another man's plasma. In an image that will be forever burned into my hole-riddled memory – my own laughing face being eclipsed by the wide, dry-textured strokes of this bloody collaborative masterpiece.

We drank a beer, dipping our fingers in to moisten the discharged corner of the slop, signing our names like famous artists, belching victorious laughter.

The next day I looked worse. Blood on flesh will dry and quickly flake away with some effortless scratching, maybe some getting caught in your three-day-old stubble on the way down. But in just twenty hours you can really see the shavings they chiseled off of you! *WHAT A SIDESHOW FREAK! NOW YOU KNOW HOW BEEF JERKY IS MADE! NOW WATCH AS HE TRIES TO CALL OUT SICK TO WORK, WITH EVERY EXCUSE IN HIS SHALLOW RESERVES ALREADY USED THREE TIMES OVER!!!*

I had to report to the theater at 4:00 that afternoon. Months earlier I had already used the immaculate alibi of "someone swinging open a door on my face" the day after I put ten stranger's cigarettes out on my forehead, in an effort to get them to leave my apartment. That lie and that stunt were successful! But the damage was too specific this time. You don't look this way from a door unless it was an iron maiden. But I could still walk, and I could still push a broom, and somewhere through my swollen eye's tear blurred outlook I bet I could still catch a glance or two at Cecilia. I could only hope without looking too much like a lost dog. I could say my eye was in throes of spasm and it was helpful for me to concentrate on a single focal point, but I feared her red hair may prove indistinguishable from the blood swirling in my corneas.

I drove straight to work like a *bukkakied* nun returning to Church. I walked through the double doors having to look down – not out of shame, but as an attempt to hide my still drunk dripping smirk. Everyone noticed but didn't want to say anything, invoking that hybrid emotion of fear and pity. Everyone except Lusterlatke.

"What the fuck happened to you man?" he said, with nearly a trace of genuine sympathy.

"I got in a pretty good fight..." I started, but by the time everyone within an earshot heard this and finally felt comfy enough to walk over to hear what happened, Lusterlatke decided he would not be upstaged. He used a slight pause from me as a springboard into an avalanche down some of the most tall-tale climbs of phony bravado I have ever heard from a human being in my life – a bar room brawl with multiple men twice his size, somehow segueing into his brief flirtation with punk rock slam-dancing. "Man, back then you had to be tough to get into one of those things!" he said, but I was not listening. Early into his shameless bloviating I saw her coming down the stairs, stopping dead on the second to last step. She zeroed in on my worked over face, jaw slowly dropping as wide as her eyes, which were now locked with mine. I watched as her look of terror slowly morphed into a teetering guilty smile, biting her lip again as she slowly looked me up and down.

FOUR

"Cockroach males practice courtship rituals, such as posturing and stridulation. Stridulation is the act of producing sound by rubbing together certain body parts. This behavior is mostly associated with insects but other animals are known to do this as well, such as a number of species of fish, snakes and spiders. The mechanism is typically that of one structure with a well-defined lip, ridge, or nodules (the "scraper" or plectrum) being moved across a finely-ridged surface (the "file" or stridulitrum—sometimes called the pars stridens) or vice-versa, and vibrating as it does so, like the dragging of a phonograph needle across a vinyl record..."

There were two impressions wore into my carpet, side-to-side and each the size of a grapefruit, symmetrically-centered in front of my stereo system. These were my knee-prints, where I kneeled religiously. I would play blues and death-rock records incessantly, focusing on every nuance and emotional reverberation inside their countless revolutions. But this new devotion went far beyond my obsession with music, as the songs I chose to spin were strictly hymns to her, and I soon realized that every song I played was written about her, and at my most far gone, written for me, by her. There were nights I would chose to stay home from the bar just so I could repeat these schizoid consolations, as I would open my window to let the cold night into my warmth, in exchange for wafting these love songs in her direction.

It took me about a year into working at the theater before I realized that I wasn't the only one infatuated with Cecilia. It was subtle
as a cat with its eye on the door, then pretending to wash itself when
you called its bluff. Every other man in that place had a thing for her
but wouldn't admit it to a tree. We all just went on as if we were in
psychic prayer booths having our private vague moments with her,
most likely existing exclusively in our own minds. No doubt the
others loved to hear her laugh as much as I did, and would use any
moment to trigger her ecstatic outbursts, ones that would end in a
smile that was so beaming it was almost painful to accept. Her
punctuating sighs reverberated in our veins. And if there were a
mutual approval of any kind of cultural ephemera, we would perceive it as a trophy that we thought to be so precious that it was our
first instinct to hide it. That is, if its very shine hadn't been reflecting
off our faces for everyone else to see. We had long since given
ourselves away.

One who showed admiration in his own special way was Lusterlatke himself, who chose to show off his sadistic, displaced prowess
by making her cry. In one of the only times I have ever wanted to
kill a man, I walked outside to the patio where she was on her hands
and knees scrubbing the grout between the tiles, Lusterlatke cast a
cold shadow over her in the unforgiving afternoon sun, screaming at
her regarding some trivial spot she missed the day before. She made
a brave attempt fighting against the flood until she saw me standing
there, nerveless. She burst into tears, running into the theater with
nothing but darkness to muffle her cries. Our tyrant threw his arms
up, cursing before noticing me there by the ivy, and like every person we've ever known who processes guilt through cold-blooded
aggression, he found a way to scold me as he ran after her into the
lobby. I waited a few seconds around the corner before I sprinted
after Lusterlatke, seeing Jimmy and others gaining towards the concession stand, towards Cecilia who was frantically gathering her

things. Before anyone could get a response out of her, she was already outside revving her engine.

We all stood there in the dimly lit lobby, paralyzed and ashamed. We all had an eye on each other, our glares asking muffled questions until Lusterlatke's sociopathic tic broke the necessary tension with his famous *chop-chop* clap as if nothing was wrong.

"ALL RIGHT! SHOWTIME EVERYBODY! We open in two minutes!!!"

I was ordered to take her place in the box office that night. I felt a closeness to her as I mimicked her beaming cordiality the best I could, but thinking of her barreling home with tears streaming down her cheeks could only contort my face into the saddest man in the world, which I saw reflecting back at me against the glass, superimposing itself on each and every customer, no matter how glad they were to be there.

A man like Lusterlatke, who had admitted on more than one occasion that he actually couldn't have given less of a shit about silent movies, even going as far as to call the genre annoying when he so eloquently exclaimed "I mean seriously, who wants to READ a fucking movie?!?!" It's important that some insight is given into his enthusiasm for opening the theater everyday, and more specifically his use of the word "SHOWTIME" before he ordered us to swing open the doors. When the man would utter this, it had less to do with the movie itself and much more to do with the certain hideous ritual he had concocted to create an *atmosphere* – only coming across as more of an accidental initiation for the audience into this tart's insincere psyche. As our ninety-year old organ player would start into the intro of our tyrant's own *original* entitled "The Silent Picture Show", Lusterlatke would take the stage with one of those stupid Shure Super 55 Elvis mics while donned in his Newsie cap and hounds-tooth pants, and yes, that same out–of-fashion-in-any-era copyrighted "Silent Movie Theater" sweatshirt rounding out his costume of supreme mockery, not so much singing as he was talking sing-songy, only in such a way that it couldn't even qualify as camp. He was, in fact, singing to these people in the designated technique one would use to express himself to a toddler with Down's Syndrome.

"Heading to the Silent Picture Show
I was born too late to ever go... oh, oh, oh
But still we get our chance
Bask in the radiance
Of the stars in the silent picture show..."

As this would go on, we had a ritual of our own. Like catty rats we would all scurry out into the lobby while the packed theater gawked, shaking our heads, rolling our eyes, dancing mockingly with Al Jolson jazz hands at this failed musician's hold out for some kind of day-late crowd gratuity, and lucky for him it happened to be in the comfort of an arena where applause was mandatory instead of inspired. Now, there are those that have failed to succeed, and then there are those who have failed to *secede*. A large reason why we remained under the tyranny of this incognizant goon is because we were hiding, seeking shelter in a dark theater while the modern world just went on living without us, reasons all varied and twisted but we had confessed this to ourselves and each other, as often as we called Charles Lusterlatke the biggest prick we had ever encountered in our lives.

I joyfully exhaled like someone's first cigarette out of jail when I saw Cecilia walk in the next day. I had convinced myself that her tear-streamed face wasn't going to look back when she drove off. Sadly, she was even less approachable, this time not from the intimidation of beauty but from a reserved mourning that had taken her over. It would be strange and maybe even controversial to hug her, so I gave her the most sincere look I could conjure, one that expressed as much sympathy as it did anger and shame. A soldier's glare. She reciprocated from across the room with a slow nod and a puzzling one-syllable whisper into the air that still to this day I have never deciphered.

It was a challenge to remember that Cecilia had a boyfriend, and it was nearly impossible to leave my gentle but persistent pining. It was the most unaffectionate union I had ever seen. Even whizzing past the typical suffocating of passions one might impose when dating someone in the workplace; this stiffness and lack of spark I just knew would carry them all the way to their doorstep and remain like a sad phantom of impotence. I would look at them and just imagine what it was like at home – John Boy with his model trains and taxidermy bug collections in all his overgrown adolescent oblivion, Cecilia on the windowsill with a Highball, rolling her eyes as she looked out longingly for some means of escape. Through this daydreaming she remained to me somehow available, singular, untainted by any ambiguous pre-mature domestic shackle, whether she or he or anyone besides me acknowledged it. But I was too painfully polite to take what was clearly mine, my reverence for this creature diluting the *conquering gene* in my DNA that had possessed me a million times before, for lesser rewards. "But it's going to be a long life" my formerly suicidal brain would whisper, where once this would trigger the urge to self-destruct in gradual but determined attempts, I would now use this an excuse to defiantly stall, to a boiling point, where no one could deny me.

FIVE

"As early as the 1940s it was reported that female Emerald Wasps species sting a cockroach (specifically a Periplaneta americana, Periplaneta australasiaeor, Nauphoeta rhombifolia) twice, delivering venom... the wasp stings precisely into specific ganglia of the roach. It delivers an initial sting to a thoracic ganglion and injects venom to mildly and reversibly paralyze the front legs of its victim. Often with its hind legs still working, this will occasionally send the roach into a panicked, confused running backwards in small circles."

I was forgetting to act my own age. Still young yet pre-maturely senile, living in the burnt out rock n' roll Armenian district of Hollywood with all its chipped paint creating shadows pointing fingers down dark alleys, beckoning me to make off-beaten path maps in my dormant heart – avenues that could allow my blood to flow through rather than the clogged uphill battles of teasing, unrequited love from impossible women that I could just as well obsess over while getting my rocks off, smearing my face all over whatever part of the atmosphere the billboards had not yet stolen. No shadows of impending gentrification were going to freeze us barnacles of the boulevard who would only move when no one was looking. Like dying but determined soldiers, out of ammo, instead turning our glass bottle bayonets on ourselves in absurd benumbing protest. I picked up right where I left off before that holy woman had entered my life, making no distinction between my apartment and the street, between moments of pant-pissing intoxication and ones of revelatory clarity, morphing the meanings of safe and sorry into a single naked display of blind adventure that turned every distant monster into a close comrade, whose names I would never remember. The smog of the day would remain as the fog of night, creating a reflective lid on this sprawling Petri-dish that would send all the lonely fluorescence right back down at us in competition with the erratic helicopter searchlights hunting for their prey.

There was a hierarchy to the landscape, which in itself is not native to Los Angeles but unique for its blatancy! While it's to be expected that the well-off live in castles in the hills that cast shadows on the rest of us, the foothills accommodating boutiques and restaurants that seemed more like museums with no culture or sense of history. Down by our more slithering section of the 101, there was proof alone in its own unassuming overpasses. Contrasted to the ones in the Franklin Hills that were carefully covered in tarp-lined chain-link tunnels that would give one the confidence to cross from one side to the other; as you got further down to our seedy section you would notice these phase out, being demoted to mere handrails, before finally retarding to thigh-high suicide friendly booby traps that were screaming reminders of the "what-if" temptation to take the plunge, should there not be the constant paranoia of that silhouette approaching you that could push you off with little to no effort.

The experiment was too real. Escape was reality and everything seemed to exist in a vacuum in-between passing out at double features, wandering the streets, and frequenting The Blacklite, a breed of bar that was slowly becoming extinct. It was at the crossroads of the curious district of Santa Monica and Western where at night it felt like Jean Genet's *Querelle* filmed on *Sesame Street* in Tijuana. After you hit yourself in the face with the plastic walk-in cooler flaps at the door, the depression would hit you like a stifling wind. The kind of place where showing up sober was out of the question, otherwise you would be all too aware of the bartender staring at you in suspicion and everyone else trying to ignore you. If you could get past this initial chill, you would carry on with your drinking only to notice everyone else that walked through that threshold probably had the same smeared, exhausted expression as you did, be it the transvestites or random *paisas*, who, just like Jack and I, were looking for a place to escape from a city we moved to because we were trying escape from everything else. There was always a heavy sigh as if to say, "Finally. And if this is all I get, so be it!"

One night Jack and I walked in just a little too sober for flowing conversation. We sat in total silence, drinking slow as we battled internal conflicts as petty as "jukebox or beer" and we were too bored to even survey the room for a way out of each other's stagnant company. We understood one another when we assumed this position – it was only awkward for others in our presence. I would always tell him, "A friend is someone that doesn't mind shutting the fuck up every once in a while..." that is, to experience the moment fully, unmolested by any phantom pressure to "turn up the night" as the billboards suggested. We knew steady, determined drinking was the only way to the destination, so we left each other alone unless there was something really Earth-shattering to say, or at the least some tidbit to ponder to keep us from nodding off.

"Jack..."

"Yeah."

"I've got it bad, man." I said with a couple heavy nods.

"Oh... A chick, huh? Anyone I know?"

"No, hopefully there's no way you would. She runs with a different crowd than us. I'm pretty sure she's got money. Kinda seems like a Bret Easton Ellis character, so I think she likes bad boys too. Someone at work said she was a child actress at one point. But fuck all that – you should see her face. Even when she's not around it seems to take up my whole periphery…"

"Oh, so you see her in our ugly fucking bartender right now? She's obviously magical. A miracle worker!" he jabbed with a chuckle.

"Man, it's like I'm fucking possessed. It's embarrassing to admit. She gives me that teenage feeling. I don't know where it comes from…"

"Man, oh man… Nostalgia, huh? What do you need that for? We're here, right now. No way out. Drink your fucking beer!"

"All right…" I said, as I took a long swig, "but I want you to think back to when you were a teenager for a second."

"Okay…" he laughed, wondering where this was going.

"Where did you think you would be right now?"

He thought for a second, then smiled almost guilty, knowing too quick what his response would be.

He shrugged, "For real? Some place just like this. Doing exactly this. I always had a feeling everything I ever did would just lay out the red carpet for this kind of purgatory. But you know what that makes me, right?"

"What's that?'

"A fucking prophet!" He slammed his glass down to punctuate as our laughter jarred the stale silence of the bar. He turned up his nose and did his best impersonation of a refined gentleman, swirling his swill to check the sudsy legs going down, "And who besides me can claim such a distinction?" he guffawed, "what about you man?" he asked.

I bit my lip and smiled ponderingly before I realized I had been

silent for too long. This question, rhetorical as it may be, always re-
quires a certain mental machete to hack through all the thickets of
petty regrets; before you realize that the here and now is the only
thing that matters. That is, if we could somehow inherit the callous-
ness to ignore the drag queen with a tattooed tear sitting next to us
crying his eyes out.

We both looked over to this creature God forgot. The build of a
football player, miraculously crammed into a skin-tight red mini
skirt that left nothing to the imagination, except for pursuing the
motives behind the Betty Boop tattoo on his bicep. Had he been
stood up or was he hiding from someone? Had he done something
that he was ashamed of, this image of jelly-glazed downcast humili-
ation? His dripping face was buried in his big sob-muffling palms,
so he could not see us stare. We did not feel guilty for our voyeurism, just suspended in a helpless empathy that rendered us motion-
less, though far from emotionless.

We refused to bear it any longer. Jack and I turned to each other,
whispering and slyly signaling with our heads to the mess beside us.
Alcohol was softening us as we decided we weren't just going to let
this grown man in red stilettos cry to nobody. We wanted to reach
out in strange un-chartered ways that might even surprise us; but
before we could make a move, he made a sudden gallop to the
jukebox like a little light went on inside his dim wounded brain. He
plunged into his purse for change and made the thing work, select-
ing a heart-wrenching ranchero ballad that soon filled up the room.
He stared into the lights of the machine and began to slowly sway
before getting the nerve to face the rest of the room to continue his
brave dance of private consolation.

We knew what had to be done. We drained our beers, got up off
of our stools and made our way to the jukebox. Before long, we also
began to sway, though careful to avoid eye contact until he knew we
were friendly and weren't going to hurt him. Soon the three of us

were dancing in universal ineptitude, occasionally ricocheting into each other and every time we did, we saw him smile and almost laugh through his tears. This went on for six more songs and that many more rounds until he took turns crying right onto our shoulders, still mournfully cursing in Spanish hysterics. When I woke up at noon the next day my collar was still damp.

All my internal hounding made me forget that Cecilia had a boyfriend. But another oversight on these prolonged stretches of debauched wanderings; I forgot that I *technically* had a girlfriend as well, though the term was as loose as my own sloppiness to put a proper end to it. Amber's phone calls managed to have the shriek of an alarm-clock, always coming to me at these deathly hung over mornings after long nights spent making myself as off the grid as flesh and blood would permit. I was a constant fugitive riding through our expired union that was already gasping under subconscious suppression. While sometimes love is a monster, ours had long become a zombie. I had given up, staying with her in theory alone, in fear that if I left she would finally follow through with her big threat of exiting the Earth.

She lived in an old hotel turned apartment building, inhabited by junkies and deserted geezers on their mutual deathbeds. While she was neither of these, she still fit right in. Once beautiful in body and spirit, by the time we met she had been corrupted by her own mind. She allowed some of the most simple kinks from her past - blood fetish, amphetamine-addiction, and a lengthy stint as a dominatrix – to become a tower of displaced guilt where it should have been a proud flag-waving testimonial that she was still breathing and still able to cast a shadow of a woman in her prime. I would have preferred that strong leather-bound, blood-sucking freak who was at least more confident in her own skin than a crying silhouette of regret, to whom sex was selfishly reduced to an act of chipping away at her low self-esteem. All of my encouragement fell to deaf ears (often due to her hands covering them) and eventually bred the death of chivalry. She planted a rare black seed of cruelty in me in which everything I shot back at her, no matter how severe, I could always find some retroactive justification. When she wasn't in sudden violent hysterics, she would assume the personality of a fragile toddler with a helium voice, her gentle weapon against me. To think, I had actually struck a child! But only after feeling the swell of my clobbered forehead, a wound she administered after one of the many times I told her I was leaving. We had become the undisputed middleweight champions of white trash love, and eventually our mutual friends evacuated our lives, leaving us only with each other. Even the cops stopped returning our calls. I was better off just disappearing for as long as I could, refusing to return home in fear of the phone ringing. But one can only hide out in public for so long. After the twenty-third ring I finally put the phone to my face.

"Hello?" I asked, as if I didn't know who it was. There was nothing but quivering sobs on the other end. "Amber! What? Talk to me!!!"

Her crying was loud, scattered, and unquenchable as a newborn, layered in thick and fluctuating rhythms. She couldn't get out more than three words at a time. I immediately stopped listening or caring about the unfounded scolding that was about to be unleashed on me like a pack of retarded coyotes. She finally made out something ear piercing if not coherent.

"YOU GET OVER HERE RIGHT NOW!!!" she said, before trailing off to more tears, her preferred language. Her nerve would be nearly comedic if I didn't have the shuddering visual of her weeping all night until her eyes were near swollen shut, volcanoes of acne erupting against the will of her Tetracycline. Laying in a riot of dirty laundry, prescription bottles, and half-eaten Thai take-out.

"YOU sound SO beautiful AND mature!!!! I will be right fucking over!!!"

I slammed the phone down so hard it rang the little bell inside. I took it as a divine symbol that this was to be the last round, whether she was ready or not, whether I could get my equilibrium to answer, whether this dizzying fatigue would ever subside.

I could have drove, biked, hitched, or bused across Hollywood to that four story Spanish-roofed catacomb, but something made me walk through the steady drizzle of rain – not to prolong the inevitable, but to really bask in the churning slime of my own venom, slow-cooking my poison so not to evaporate its potency. It was a righteous evil, the kind bred only from a well-meaning but ignorant purity, whose mind and joints and soul have slowed from the friction of martyrdom until one finally realizes the truest language is the one always denied in order to make life *easier.* The stripping of the flesh, unleashing the object of your affection's true spirit even if it is the Devil Herself, *then* confrontation!!! I had forgotten to forget that she was human.

I approached the Vietmanese Bakery with the full-color poster in the window advertising their *blood soup special.* I had passed this on the way to her place a billion times before, but in this moment, my stomach churned the hungry way. I turned right onto the corner of Vine and Lexington, the intersection I longed to be unfamiliar with. There stood the dust-caked Lexington Hotel, a dim red light making her third story apartment glow dull in the grey wash of the afternoon's storm. The lobby door was open, thanks to the arched back of one of its older tenants leaning against it, slowly swaying with every oblivious nod-out, cigarette in hand long extinguished. I walked passed him and spared the pleasantries as I began to stomp up the first flight of stairs, skipping two, sometimes three steps all the way up, gaining momentum with each anvil leg thrown.

Arriving at her door my hand went straight for the knob in lieu of the knock. *I do this because we are not strangers, yet soon we will be* I thought. The door swung open, the door she suspiciously kept all three locks and deadbolt on day and night, the gate to her lair that was opening into a crimson-tinged darkness before me.

She materialized from stage left, light from the hallway harshly exposing her in her one-strap-off-white slip as she slowly stumbled toward me like a fawn just learning to walk. Her head down in shame, dyed black hair shrouding the wrists she was rubbing into her eyes to dam the tears. She stopped a foot away, lifting her head just enough to reveal her pout, lips quivering in sing-songy abused child voice. "Where…Where did you go?" as dumb and innocent as if we had been playing a game of hide and seek, as though the last explosion down the wires never happened.

"Nowhere, sweetheart. I have always been here. In fact I think I have been here too long. I have to say goodbye now. Now and for good. Goodbye now."

I forgot to forget she was human again. That shitty brittle orphan voice had pried itself under my skin and burrowed into my veins, contaminating the blood in my heart and my hand as I ceremoniously touched her shoulder one last time when I should have just back-handed the words right out of her B-movie mouth. Not a second wasted, she threw her hand on top of mine in dominance - not desire - quickly grabbing my forearm with her other hand and began climbing into me, using my flesh as a way to crawl out of her own pit. It wasn't long before we were using my arm in a tight-wound game of tug of war. She fell to her knees for desperate leverage, pulling me down as hard as she could cry, and every time I yanked the other way she screamed like back-alley rape, her tried and true secret weapon against resistance of any sort when the baby talk failed. I got my whole body outside the door except for my left arm, where she was digging her flaking nails, half-buried into my skin. I managed to position her wrists into the door jamb and started slamming the door on them as hard as I could. There was clearly no other way I was going to get out of her sad, determined talons. I exhaled a heavy clenched-teeth breath streaked in eerie irony, as I marveled it was the second time that month I had seen this door-as-weapon technique. I gave Jack a private nod for the contagious ingenuity. *Let's not start sucking each other's dicks yet, Caleb...* I imagined him responding, as her neighbors began opening their doors and coming out into the hallway with gaping looks of phony concern, more annoyed we were killing their own private buzz.

"What are you doing to her?!?" some catatonic prick inquired.

"Mind your own fucking business!!!" I barked damply, giving equal pressure to the door onto her elbow as I struggled to break away from her grasp. I noticed some others down the hall eyeing us while beginning to dial their phones. Again.

The pressure was on both of us now. I resorted to placing my foot on the hallway wall for added leverage, and as I gave one last yank I heard her scream as her splintered nails carved bloody trails down my arm, the door slamming shut with a quickly diminishing echo down the hall, a bellowed draft stinging my new wounds.

"NO! NO! NO! Nooohohoho..." she howled her disapproval from the other side. I heard the door creak open again but I was already half-way down the hall, passing each dumb neighbor as their bulging eyes zeroed in on my slaughtered forearm. I wide-curved the corner and jumped the whole first flight of stairs like a firefighter on the way to a call, though I was already ill with adrenaline from the one I had just extinguished. Instead of looking back, I shuffled home imagining her whole building reduced to blackened heaps of smoldering cinders; with maybe some clues left scattered across the charcoal-smeared foundation that showed glaringly what truly negligent tenants they all were. There were no survivors.

SIX

"The roach's temporary loss of forward mobility paves the way for the wasp's second and most moribund sting into the roach's head ganglia, or brain – specifically the area that controls the escape reflex. As a result, the roach will first groom extensively, then become sluggish and fail to show its normal lightning speed escape responses… All considered by researchers as the roach's 'zombie state' once the wasp gains full control of the roach's will."

O ur nights at the theater became tauntingly long. Lusterlatke's bread and butter was whoring out the place for special events, accepting any function held by anyone, as long as the cash wasn't counterfeit. The Scientologists and the Deep-Valley Porn Moguls were repeat customers in between all the coffin-enclosed gothic weddings, has-been autobiography signings, unattended C-movies, spoiled brat birthdays and assorted other dredge that could turn a historical landmark into a cake-smeared, spilled red Solo cup, too drunk to drive, sequin scattered, glitter begotten dumping ground in a matter of hours. We were there to shut up and suck up. The more trashcans we provided, the more guests would fumble their disposals and accidentally do *The Twist* in their spilled cupcake. It seemed the only ones to have any respect, self-awareness or panoramic view of their own path were those well on their way to their natural deathbeds.

Ironically, the porn industry gatherings were the most down-to-earth of the offenders. They had all either seen each other naked or actually fucked each other for money, so there was no one left to impress with sex being conveniently already out of the way. This left nothing but smiles and genuine intelligent conversation, even with us servers. Paired with sneaking drinks from the bar, this made those otherwise long nights fly. One night Jimmy gave them a special treat for their humble patronage – after scouring the vaults he had emerged with a reel of silent porn from the 30s and screened it for the party. Lusterlatke was elsewhere hobnobbing so we peeked in. Like skin flicks of today it left nothing to the imagination, but it was not what you would call sexy by modern standards. Both actors seemed to be enjoying themselves, but with polite, toothy grins in the throes of an act which resembled a neighborly favor, rather than any mutual passionate outpouring. The men seemed content and dutiful as spraying the final wash of suds off their car and the gals faces looked as though they were getting their hair done. No one was getting hurt. Perhaps we really have de-evolved.

These nights would end with us either having to race to the bar down Fairfax for last call, or indecisively kicking our heels at the ground until someone would finally offer up their house so we could go erase the evening together. One night Jimmy offered up his pad not too deep in the Valley.

"All right, that's it, we're going to my house! Al Jolson double-feature, how's that sound? I bet no one here has seen *Wonderbar*? Oh man…" he said as he shook his head with a malevolent smirk, "HA! There's no way they would green light this movie these days! It's beyond just blackface! That's all I'm gonna say, don't ask me any questions. We're going…"

And so the caravan began.

Jimmy's apartment was just at the bottom of that first decline entering North Hollywood off the 101. A cinephile of the highest order, he had arranged his apartment into a makeshift theater, complete with projector and white pullout screen, its sides matted with black borders for definition. Within five minutes of the lights going out, you would forget where you were. Enveloped in darkness, we could barely make out the windows or the outside world unless the moon happened to be creeping by. The only problem was adequate seating. Jimmy wasn't used to having this many people over, so we all kind of landed in the first place our eyes happened to capture. John Boy oddly made himself the martyr on a stool when any man in his right mind would have found a place next to his beautiful woman. Why, he could have taken her by the hand and led her to the floor, where they could lay arm in arm assuming the spot they left off in their own little world!!! Did they have a little world? I had more of a world with that woman even if it had not been consummated by any physical contact beyond the tangible pressure of our eyes locking, so heavy I always had to look away. I grabbed the first spot on the right of the wide-open couch, which everyone was too polite to claim. Merel followed suit with the left side, and as if there was a crescendo in the orchestration of the cosmos, Cecilia squeezed herself right in the middle of us, an exposed thigh from her denim mini-skirt oozing into the knuckles of my fingers which gripped the corner of the cushion so tight like I was about to take off in a rocket ship.

My eyes darted down at this unintentional contact of bony digits to pillowing flesh, as that lucky electric current shot up my arm and neck before exploding into my head into what I refer as *champagne brain*, an internal effervescence that challenged as well as reaffirmed my very existence. A benevolent army of delicate bubbles swabbed a numbing, narcotic trail up my spine, popping playfully off the top of my head. Only for that split second of each burst would I feel myself again before another countless amount would already be halfway through their ascent. I struggled in vain to keep my eyes open but the feeling was far too strong. If my two eyes could have a slurring dialogue between each other, that moment they admitted a conjoined defeat. They closed gently with the pride of someone that had just shown off their favorite possession kept in a special box, the privilege of the viewing mutually understood.

There was no telling how long I fell asleep for, but the movie was well along. I was awoken by the sound of brass, carrying a montage of Jolson in blackface riding a mule to heaven where there was dancing watermelon and fried chicken celebrating his arrival. I looked to my left just in time to see her laugh uproariously while her thigh had remained still, if not pressed harder against me.

John Boy had assumed his own subtle reverse racist caricature, a white boy so captivated by dancing fruit that he was oblivious to the heat his woman was effortlessly generating, slowly melting me into the cushions. He stared at the screen slack-jawed, slapped his forehead with a gurgle, then fingered the screen as he turned his shaking head at me to say, "Can you believe it?"

I could not.

The next day I realized I was beginning to not only despise, but actually fear my days off - or any time I was left alone for that matter – as any and all thoughts would quickly lead back to her, her image, voice and her place in my occupied mind. All of the hypothesis, every midnight fantasy and every tiny crumb of half-baked rationale was just as torturous as worshipping a brick wall. Every harmless cliché of love took on systematically cruel proportions, though grid-like and ever connecting – everything I came into contact with somehow reminded me of her, all objects offering direct clues or becoming instant souvenirs of time spent musing on her. Even conversations overheard in public seemed littered with people talking about her as well. Bits of chatter would complete obsessive epigrams I intended only for myself to hallucinate and make real rungs of a ladder, which I hoped would either lead me to her or to my previous life where I was actually in control. I knew I was in trouble when it was eight pm and realized I had heard Lesley Gore's "I Will Follow Him" three whole times that day, all in different parts of the city. To me, that song was always the anthem of obsession at its most psychotic and self-reducing worst. Every time I heard it I could only imagine gaggles of women with knives stabbing downwards to the rhythm of "I love him! I love him! I love him!" The fact that the genders were reversed had no weight on my pride in relating reluctant to the tune, as I had become considerably emasculated since I was surrounded, in the middle of some strange body of water that was Cecilia. I was frantically treading in circles like a cockroach tangled in tissue, looking for the solid porcelain shores of the toilet.

The next week marked a substantial decline for Cecilia and John Boy. We noticed him missing days at work. She refused to comment on the subject, or much of anything else. She walked in a one-woman procession without the luxury of a veil, looking straight ahead or down but never eye contact with any of us. There was nothing I could do but continue to be a silent witness to the mystery when I wasn't walking in on her confiding in someone she felt more comfortable with, pretending like I didn't know what was going on even though everyone was guardedly muttering.

It was Sunday afternoon and intermission was to start in five minutes. Cecilia and I were assigned to the coffee bar in the patio while the others stood by the doors in the lobby. I watched her sweep the tiles by the ivy, occasionally stopping to twist the tendrils into her fingers and thumb, before tangling them into the other vines to train. The sun was hitting her so completely that I felt a twinge of guilt for a girl that was holding so much inside, yet so exposed.

She turned around in time to notice me watching. Now I was exposed. Her solemn face did not change though the direction of her path did, now walking toward where I stood behind the bar. Looking down as she walked, she reached the halfway point, raising her head to make eye contact, as if to be assured I was still watching her. This time I did not look away. Her head returned its attention to the path in front of her. As she got close enough to touch the bar with her left hand, she brought herself around to my side behind it. Not a word spoken, she lifted herself onto the bar and oozed into a leisurely lean, one leg dangling off in a pendulum's sway.

"You okay there?" I asked.

"Yeah... I mean, yeah?" She smiled vacantly with a sigh until her last word dissolved into regret, and went on, "John Boy and I broke it off."

"Oh. I'm sorry. I had a feeling."

"No, no don't be sorry."

We paused for so long I was almost crushed in the vice of the tightening moment. I continued to pry in spite of my guts gurgling into my mouth, as they had nowhere else to go besides the malfunctioning washing machine of my stomach.

"Can I ask what happened?"

She sighed again and shook her head, "It's a little... Personal? I mean, I don't really mind telling you. You two guys barely even knew each other..."

She was cut off by the intermission crowd pouring in to crawl all over our fresh canvas, these forgettable creatures in leisurewear who were none the wiser, as one by one they approached her and I at the bar, somehow delighted to see us.

Supposedly, Boy Howdy was a real monster. If there is one thing we were told, it is that one should never trust an amateur taxidermist that only goes after creatures smaller than him. She wanted normal and boring and she got domestic abuse, which in many worlds is normal, boring... We always wondered what the hell went on after they left work every night, how the story would go on without the rest of us, leaving a not only unlikely but nonsensical couple to whatever kind of life they lead in their $3000 a month three-story house. They couldn't afford a place like this on theater peanuts alone. Each to their own isolated nooks, miraculously lonely worlds of lint-caked craftsmanship and pet stained carpet between them in this house they could no longer maintain through charade. Would one of them retire to bed mournfully after the other? The downstairs couch began to leave an impression of his lanky body. But somewhere in this doused rehearsal of settling down - much too forced, premature, and too stillborn to even register as anything funereal. He had choked her on more than one occasion, and not the kinky stuff that we might hope two people with some exciting sexual transgressions might try. It always went down when Cecilia would request she be left alone for the night. Then there was some kind of still-steaming iron to the face, supposedly thrown from a close distance. There were a lot of blanks begging to be filled but I had stopped listening. My head was a goddamn Gravitron, though it took brief breaks from spinning where I would be too dizzy to want to kill the man. After all, it was just she and I now, laying deep in the ivy on the side of the 101, lusciously bombed as she spilled her guts in steady generous drips.

I knew it was after midnight because the rhythmic whiz of cars on the freeway had graduated to Saturday night traffic hours ago and now it was a sparse free-for-all as we heard the creeping *wooosh* every five seconds or so, reminding us of our strange setting - a guy and girl, dressed sharp though blowsy, lounging on our elbows in the debris dusted vines, too comfortable to look like accident victims in this slice of no-man's land. We chose this spot due to its hybrid clash of obviousness and neglect, a place you pass in a car and think, "There's that place where nothing happens again." Los Angeles is riddled with these voids of possibility. Every so often I would check on the stumbling shadows of homeless setting up camp against the tree a couple yards away, before accepting them as part of the scenery, silent witnesses to the end of my lifetime of a day.

It started when Cecilia gave me a ride home at before midnight, only I had her drop me off a block away so I could buy cigarettes at the corner store. I walked to my place and quickly realized I did not have my keys after doing a spastic pat down. She had driven off and neither of us had cell phones, nor did I have her number. I was handed the vagabond card. I called Jack on a payphone and we closed out the Blacklite. We went back to his apartment and stayed up all night with his rocker neighbors who were successfully living out some depraved Sunset Strip fantasy, shooting speed with a scant-clad Filipino who told us she was a prostitute, the younger sister of one of the main shot callers at The Smogcutter. I drank their Jager-meister. I passed out on his couch while they played *Hanoi Rocks* records at a criminal volume.

The next morning I arrived at the theater with my accustomed hangover, the familiar pain in all my vitals, and creeping paranoia that the whole world had my number, uncertain but tailor-made penalties awaiting me around every corner.

I took a deep breath, exhaling through my rasberrying lips as I swung open the double doors, ushering in a gust of wind with my arid constitution. I glanced to the right as I stepped into the cross-road of the lobby. The more fertile, feral population of the theater's crew was in a conspicuous huddle, muffled chortles with transparent back-turned fingers across mouths. They turned to me red faced then quickly turned away before Cecilia's mocking voice put only the loosest lid on the commotion.

"Oh Caaaaaleb…?"

She cried out to me in a sort of bratty clairvoyance as if she knew something I didn't, wanting not just to make sure I knew, but that there was an audience of people present whose menstrual cycles were in synch to the second. My stomach plummeted to a splash of memories from adolescence where there had been quivering cabals of females wanting my head. Warranted or not, no one conspires and wins like women you have loved. But before I could fully relinquish my stature, now in near hunch from this DT-fueled pressure cooking, the girls began to retreat, slowly turning, then symmetrically peeling away from the nucleus like a Busby Berkeley montage, leaving Cecilia in the crease of the Rorschach, her outstretched arm dangling my keys, making little shaky sounds as if she was telling me it was dinner time.

"You know, I was looking at these… There's a really interesting one in here… Aha! Here it is!"

She walked toward me smirking, still dangling the keys, being held from one she had chosen. It was my old apartment key, somehow never disposed of, one that had been spirally tweaked - whose teeth were chipped and jagged as a curbed carny, from something drunk, some wrong apartment, the garbage disposal or…

"Exotic," she said, starring me right into the eyes.

"Uhm, what?"

She repeated herself, only this time breathy, eyes lightly shut as her head swayed like a slow-motion shampoo commercial.

"Exotic." She nailed a hard C, which triggered her eyes back open. She was of course referring to my key, one only she could grant an erotic sainthood. I exploded with a case of severe catalepsy while feeling I had been robbed of all my clothing. It was only she and I left in the lobby and no longer did I want to run.

There we were in the ivy on the side of the freeway amidst layers of yellowed newspaper and knotted weed, passing the wine like a lazy metronome, saluting each passing car with every reciprocated swill. It occurred to me in this darkness that she was just as overwhelmed by our orbit, now frighteningly near collision. With each hearty sip we were not quenching our thirst so much as we were surrendering our white skins to the embrace of the umbra, knowing this was the only solace where we could forge our path without threat of some ignorant appraisal from our peers. She knew, just as well as I did, that the world was as savage as it was unabashedly in love with her.

We emerged from the invulnerable void to our neon runway with a dauntless stride, using the tips of our feet as divining rods to the obvious destination – my black hole of an apartment. Without a word spoken we signed the initiations of a secret if not silent language. We walked up the steps as though we both lived there together for years. No questions. No answers. No skin crawling squirms to wonder what we were supposed to be doing once we entered. I quietly opened the door, not wanting to skip the perfect soundtrack of our footsteps walking in, finally becoming real. My ghetto-esque sheet covering the window had popped a tack, allowing the moon to beam in through the imperfections of the bent blinds, so I didn't bother with the light. Instead, I continued to my bed without feeling any need to look behind me. I made myself horizontal, fully clothed and facing the wall, until I felt her weight on the bed, using the momentum of her sinking into the mattress to fall

all over her. As I slowly reached over into embrace, I saw her two hands join together to her chest, genuflecting, communicating the same holiness I had been fiending to scream while allowing me to receive her completely.

We awoke like proud fugitives the next morning, feeling as if the second we would pull our arms asunder the dream would fade. So we stayed in bed laughing greedily, devising plans, acknowledging dangers of our mission and how to make this all invisible, save for us. Our workplace was a landmine of potential broken hearts, middle-aged misplaced jealousy, and young adults far too inexperienced to deal with this - any and all could rob it of its reverence. They would call it Satanic, the way we were sacrificing innocent flesh by splicing alternate endings into everyone's reels. "Fuck off!" I proclaimed to them, "You cannot argue with a bona fide chef, who has brought you a slow-cooked meal with the patient love of his watchful eye rather than running across the street to bring you a burger just because your stomach is empty from your own lack of guts! We had earned this coaxial heist! How could one even have some pertinent protest when two people, fiercely independent of you, have already made the decision?!? Is there any other perfect way to remind a crybaby that they are no longer part of the equation? To the orphanage! We will babysit you only when we are not catching each other's eyes across the room like we did so many times before, only now we *know* we are ALLOWED!" I stood on the bed giving my speech as she laughed heartily.

We watched nature go nuts outside my window, one of those rare L.A. climacterics where the wild wind reminds us that nothing is really bound to Earth beyond scientific theory. Palm trees were bending, nearly kissing the ground, finally fed up with being too high and lonely all that time. Random trench-coated figures walked in a ten o'clock lean, fighting a horizontal gravity like soldiers in a hail of bullets. Palm fronds did erratic dances, flying through the air like exotic birds with brain damage, eventually being swallowed up by the funereal asphalt, though their teeth would later pop a thousand tires in rigor mortis revenge. The world seemed unbearably naked and biblical! We were teetering on chimerical panic, and if there was one thing I ever learned about the abyss, and feeling like you're about to die, is to jump right into it laughing, egging on its passing power. We split from my cinerarium and returned into the fire of public. My stomach did that thing again as I took the record needle off. We shut the door behind us as we made our way through the back gate into the alley, looking both ways for any spying birds with loose beaks. We dove into her car before I had a chance to clear the windshield of palm frond debris, so I hit the wipers as we laughed, watching them fall again. Only these alleged benign flora could signify an absurd takeover, as they possess the only leaf that takes the whole branch with it in its independent sound-mind suicide, growing more calcareous as it rots rather than turning so meek it flakes into dust like all the other jumpers that were not strong enough to hold on until the bad weather passed. They remain where they land, communicating a special obscenity to the world by their mere existence, much like Cecilia and I were. The periphery had become a massive crater, where even on solid ground the city could swallow us up, all asphalt molten lava.

"So, where shall we go?" I asked, surrendering all possibilities to her wide reply.

"I am kidnapping you." she stated matter of fact, somehow serene.

"But the victim can not be willing for it to qualify as such."

"Right." she concurred, "and nor are you a kid. You are a sweet, lost dipsomaniac doggy and I have found you and now I am taking you home with me. Will that do?"

"Yes, that will do just fine." I said, as I closed my eyes in complete undiscerning approval.

We whizzed through the backstreets in an imaginary high-speed chase with the phantom eyes belonging to the armies of men who wanted her alive and me dead for having her. I had struck such gold that I felt fleeting pangs of guilt that made me trip over my own feet in victory dance, thinking of all the lonely hordes of the city that I was not only escaping, but abandoning. There was a simple remedy for this – simply looking to my left at the profile of her sly smiling full moon face, where I was reassured it was no longer my civic duty to wander without confidence.

She raced us through a residential rollercoaster of hills I never knew existed until we parked in front of her double garage. My eyes ascended to the un-humble abode, wondering which section of this three-story fortress she actually inhabited. I never knew a single person that didn't have roommates or scraped by in some slumlord neglected apartment building, until she told me the whole thing was hers. At twenty-three, she already possessed the air of a dowager. Any residual trauma of kicking out John Boy after the alleged neck ringing had seemed to metabolize rapidly, as she now had the curious confidence of a widow who's had her husband snuffed out so she can hoodwink his insurance, now free to do whatever she pleased.

To demonstrate this, she began walking up the stairs, skipping a couple steps ahead of me until she hovered at eye level. She curled her fingers softly around the end of her denim skirt and began folding it upwards, slowly in rhythm with each step, revealing the lower curve of her posterior after hinting at the heart-stopping depth of her crevice, fingers still determined to work the skirt over the tightness of her midway, until it finally all opened up like the sun at noon shining right in my eyes. I died and was quickly re-born. Still ascending the stairs, she completed this gesture of guts and goodwill by looking over her shoulder to observe my reaction. I hid my astonished stun with the most severe stare, which I aimed into the center of her pupils and nowhere else, as my mind had been immediately burned with an image I would carry with me my whole life. She responded drowsily, glancing down at her fine work and then heavily back at me, her skirt crumpled and resting like a textured twisted halo around her waist and I knew it would take a man much stronger than I to ever get it to come back down again.

Though down it came, as she ballerina tip-toed her calf-bulging final lift to the last step. The ritual concluded as she shimmied back into chastity, only now overflowing with an anxious dormancy. Her skirt had taken on a mystical role, somehow remaining obscene whether it concealed flesh or gradually disappeared, revealing an ephemeral tangibility. A moral was revisited here, that a secret is more likely to retain its holy glow only if it is buried deep immediately after it has been shared. I was quickly reminded that I could offer her a secret of my own, hidden between my legs, though this one was to be buried not once, but over and over again, in to what I could only hope to be its final resting place.

She reached for the front door as I followed close behind. She continued to glance back to assure my pursuit. She turned the knob, flashing me a ghost of a smile that barely slipped past my vantage, as she turned back to guide us into her royal haven, the foreign scent of cleanliness chipping away at - yet almost asphyxiating - my tarred lungs in the throes of smog and dust withdrawal, as the door wafted the house's essence out to greet me. "Welcome, you lucky boy..." it seemed to whisper. Cecilia noticed my dumb glaze, to our left her living room with windows wide open, a cool breeze blowing the sheer curtains into playful waves. The furniture, couch, loveseat, and armchair all draped in the same vintage floral pattern and strategically placed in perfect feng shui atop a soft, deep-bristled carpet, still white and virginal. Any impending threat of stain would be dissolved airborne in its own beaming antiseptic radiance! All she had to do, which she of course serendipitously did on cue, was walk across this untouchable scene, now in nothing but a classic off-white slip which barely touched the floor as she seemed to hover off the ground in slow motion, like an apparition in the windows, where she closed each one in a careful ritual. She pensively gazed out, one hand touching the glass and slowly, thoughtlessly slipping down – a move I thought could only belong to the camp of a karaoke actress you see on the monitor – until she gave it a timeless sanctity that dreaming finally deserved. She looked back at me as though she had been caught, so she returned to my station where I had not moved, still in the mouth of her threshold. She extended her small right hand to my left, and began to guide me up three sets of stairs, where each set seemed to multiply after each plateau met, until we came to her room, her Westside wall nothing but glass – we were too high for any stone to ever reach – though it injected us with complete naked vulnerability whether we were to be clothed or not, where we could see not only the tops of buildings but the clouds profiles as well. It was then, as I realized I was paralleled with the heavens that I thought, "Now I can die."

SEVEN

"The wasp proceeds to chew off half of each of the roach's antennae. Researchers believe that the wasp chews off the antenna to replenish fluids or possibly to regulate the amount of venom because too much could kill and too little would let the victim recover before the larva has grown. The wasp, which is too small to carry the roach, then leads the victim to the wasp's burrow, by pulling one of the roach's antennae in a manner similar to a leash, each antennae dictating direction of right or left... "

We took separate cars reporting for duty at the theater the next day. We staggered our arrivals with a five-minute gap between each other to not raise suspicion. Our psychically conjoined head tempted the constant thought that everyone actually gave a shit. I walked in undetected, as she was being lambasted by Lusterlatke for being two minutes late, the rest of the crew scrambling behind them for no good reason other than his bad vibes. Everyone seemed to stare at me as if I had done something wrong as well - at least that's how I took it with the steaming euphoric egofueled paranoia of newly captured love boiling inside me. Their looks were stifled battle-worn cries for help and solidarity, like a platoon knowing well their doom, pushed to the limits of tolerance. The air inside was instantly more suffocating than usual and it gave one the feeling of panic as if something was about to happen, an explosion of pressure fermented too long. I went to the patio bar, back to the initial scene of the seeds of crime that had bloomed into our now blossomed union. Cecilia pulled out a bottle of champagne that was meant for the guests and handed it to me.

"I think you know what to do with this."

Without a word, I popped the cork. It shot through the patio onto the cement slab where some poor schizophrenic was buried; a man who kept coming back to the theater and was now doomed to remain there forever.

I took the biggest swig all those burning bubbles would allow before handing it to her, to which she immediately mimicked my fervor. We stared each other dead in the eyes as we repeated this back and forth, quick as a cockroach, swift as a wasp, and within the three minutes we had left before the private party started she was laughing as she poured the last drops into my mouth, like I was a baby bird receiving his mother's loving regurgitations.

We were downright clandestine but fuck-all drunk as the guests came piling into the patio. She and I were too busy ingesting the amenities to realize we hadn't done shit to prepare, so I stumbled into the spacious supply closet that went the whole length of the theater's right side. As I swung open the door I saw six familiar faces gasp. There was Jimmy, Merel, and the rest, clutching Styrofoam cups huddled around a bottle of whiskey, also intended for the guests.

"Oh my God! It's just you... We thought you were Lusterlatke!"

"Perish the thought, but you guys should hurry. He started letting people in."

"Caleb..." Dave started, followed by the rest...

"WE DO NOT CARE."

Uproarious laughter made us care even less.

"Well, fucking give me some then..." I half-whispered as I grabbed the bottle, layering some brown on my bubbly.

"Caleb..." Jimmy started in again. "We've all been talking. It looks like tonight's the night."

I knew exactly what he meant, as it was clearly the same thing on Cecilia and I's mind. Tonight we walk out, like we had collectively fantasized over drinks countless times. "We'll know when the time is right..." we would always say, as if the time wasn't always right... if we only hadn't loved the theater itself in such a blind sentimental death-grip.

"Oh, I know... Cecilia and I were just outside drinking our own confidence. I think we're ready." I giggled as I glared at them. They smiled back, but as corpses that wanted to die again by their own hand. On cue, Cecilia walked in, laughing at the sight of us.

"It's settled then," I declared, "the bottle stays here, but let's make sure this thing is drained by nightfall, that's another hour and a half, right when things are gonna get restless around here. Let's leave this place stumbling and never come back. We will be blackballed anyway. So take everything you own, take everything you don't own – candy, coffee, booze – whatever consumables that aren't nailed down. Everything else belongs to this hallowed ground."

We filed out and scattered while Cecilia flew in another direction to find and distract Lusterlatke, but the theater was so packed with guests that we had no trouble blending in to execute our nonchalant return. The night's special event was some kind of fundraiser for some group that was already wealthy – we could tell once we realized the bottle of champagne we had just dusted was one of the six bottles of Dom Perignon Vintage 1995 White Gold Jeroboam we were told too late to be selling for $250 for each small glass. We opened another one and hid it under the bar for just the two of us, determined to complete this path of defiance in style.

A veil of haze dripped into the remainder of the night, all memories compromised except for the only one that really mattered – the six of us squeezing ourselves into the exit chamber to kick open the front door just three hours into our shifts, so giddy, scared, and so fucking obliterated that Fairfax seemed to be quaking in our shattered kaleidoscopic triple vision. We left the theater and never came back as if it were a deceptive lover we had finally found the guts to leave.

"What if you moved in?" she asked with coy determination, "it makes me sad to think of you in that lonely place, and you know there is more space than I know what to do with… "

My stomach dropped with hybrid shock and excitement, and slight insult that I quickly smothered and forgot. Part of me possessed a large pride in my lifestyle and my environment, both direct reflections of my personality, so why would I change?

"I just know it would be so good. We could even hyphenate our last names on our mail?" she asked with a half-laugh, never mind her marble eyes so wide as she looked at me, baited, awaiting my excitement.

It was adorable enough for me to take her hand and say, "Let's do this."

The week before the move, I had been told by many that I seemed to be riding a wave of manic frivolity, making erratic decisions, willfully hemorrhaging money I didn't have, downing flasks of Jameson before applying for jobs, and "what is the deal with that fucked up tattoo?" they would ask. I would tell the fools it was to pay tribute to my former life and my new one with Cecilia but expected no one to understand. And I am not sure if *I* even understood this image on my arm - a cockroach on a crucifix, complete with dripping yellow gore from the stigmata wounds, rays of glorious sunlight shining behind it all. My fast-talking, half-Mexican, half-Italian pal Luis had just recently taken up tattooing and he needed all the practice he could get, so he waved the fee. I offered up my flesh, and Luis was at my door within a half hour. As soon as the door was open enough for him to slip inside, he headed straight for the bathroom, frantic. Shortly after, I found an emptied bottle of Nyquil in the trash, one I had just bought the night before. The deal instantly sweetened, *numbs-the-word* for this recently cleaned-up junkie, as far as anyone of us knew anyway.

We spread my bed sheet over the kitchen table after trying for five solid minutes to spray and scrub off the ancient grime that had been there since decades ago. Luis busted out his gun and gear meticulously, much like an excited dope fiend would set up his works. I silently mused on Luis' high-as-kite grin as he set up shop, laughing to myself, wondering if he really thought I was that much of an idiot. I decided against confrontation, as I was only glad he was piercing my skin instead of his own, for once. He shaved my forearm lovingly as I made a self-loathing gorilla joke. He dug the gun in hard as the room filled with the scent of plasma, blood, and Vaseline.

"So what's the deal with the roach, man?"

"Well..." I thought, "Omnipresence. They've been the one constant in my life. They've even been considerate roommates, usually making themselves scarce when I come home. And you know what else? They would never touch my Nyquil!"

I couldn't help it. Luis put his hands on his head as if to surrender.

"I'm sorry, Caleb. Look, you're getting a free cockroach on a crucifix tattoo and I'm having a bad day." I knew what he meant by bad day. I got back on subject.

"No, really though... I love the cockroach. They're my spirit animal. Survival and perseverance. They are the misunderstood patron saints of staunch independence. And what do we do? We scream, spray, or squash instead of trying to hone in on all their secrets..."

Luis smiled, nodding appropriate but perhaps not voluntary, eyes glazed from the purple syrup. "Yeeeeeeeeeeeeeeaaahhh..." he nasally whispered, "yeah, then there was that day after you OD'd on that peanut butter meth? Remember how fucking out of it you were? You forgot you had a heart! You forgot what a heart even was! We came to visit you at your folks and your hands just kept squashing your chest... Were you really convinced your irregular heartbeat was two fucking cockroaches chasing each other in a small circle? That's what you were telling us!"

I had been trying to erase the memory through the years. "Well, yeah!" I replied matter-of-factly, "I was trying to kill them. If I would press on them hard enough they would slow down and even stop for a while."

"Thaaaaaat's cause you were haaaaaaaving a heaaaaaaaaart attack!" Luis shook his head, smiling sarcastic as he poked my chest with his finger.

I was getting more desperate calls from Jack than I could keep up with, all seeped in the sentimental panic of impending surgery to sever a Siamese twin. I hadn't pushed the usual limits of neon endurance with my best friend in almost a week – a suspicious eternity for him and I. Instead, I was testing the boundaries of absence, an uncertainty that was doing nothing to inspire or excite. I decided it was no time to show off Cecilia to all the brave and dumb angels of my nightlife. The rush of being freshly captive seemed to paralyze time, making sure that perfect moment to integrate our inner circles never did come.

My last Saturday in Hollywood came quick. I shoved the last cardboard box of what Cecilia curiously kept calling my *tchotchke*. I saw my neighbors – my drinking gang of the last four years – lining up on the stoop, and never before had they made day drinking look so delicious and well, touching. They called to me like teenagers in the zero hour of summer.

"Come chill for a sec! One more drink before you leave us in the dust!" barked Johnny with mournful authority.

I had taken no more than four steps before Cecilia counter-called.

"No, thanks! We really need to get going and he's not driving with booze barreling through his veins!" she said as she laughed to cover up her thirst for something else.

They stared at her silent, confused over her decline of an invitation that wasn't exactly for her. I walked over, embarrassed to say my goodbyes. They stood proud in a firing squad form, as we practically suffocated each other with embraces, play-choking each other to divert the chance of it becoming too mushy. The girls hugged the hardest. I was only moving two miles away, but in L.A. that might as well be a different state. This moment made it feel like a different country altogether. I waved goodbye from the U-Haul with my lofty new beauty in tandem.

I looked over to her, trying to change the subject of the bittersweet severing of my old neighborhood and I.

"What is that word you keep calling all my boxes?"

"Oh! Yeah. TCHOTCHKE. You know…. Worthless stuff."

I took one more look at my old friends getting smaller in the rearview, and for a second, I felt like I was as well.

EIGHT

"While a number of venomous animals paralyze prey as live food for their young, Ampulex compressa is different in that it initially leaves the roach mobile and modifies its behavior in a unique way… Research has shown that while a stung roach exhibits drastically reduced survival instincts (such as swimming, or avoiding pain), motor abilities like flight or flipping over are unimpaired."

The house was still ridiculously oversized for two people, and furnished like some old time estate that teenagers had taken over. There was a grand piano, antique china cabinets full of expensive plates and glassware. A doily seemed to cover any square inch of exposed varnished wood grain, but underneath it all – an explosive mess. The off-white carpet was a nice shade of crimson camouflage from wine stain over wine stain, cotton stuffing sprinkled in bunches from the dog violently humping a teddy bear, a neglected graveyard of dead bugs littering the edge of the floor and the veranda window, all signs of what may have been comforts in my previous home; but I could not for the life of me define why all this space to roam and relax struck me as suffocating. I felt a mysterious vacuum suction adhering to my brain, unable to focus on anything as I began to feel pangs of guilt for all these messes I had made since arriving.

It had been about a half hour before I realized I had been aimlessly pacing around the house, picking up objects, putting them back down again. This would only be interrupted by sudden trips to the bathroom where I would compulsively comb my hair, rearranging the part-line then flipping it to where it originally was, then back. On Cecilia's urging, I had recently cut my rat's nest hair, after throwing away my two drilled cat-bones I would wear as primitive barrettes, which I was very attached to in my botched attempts to ape Screamin' Jay. I was still trying to find the right way to wear my new clean-cut coif. I even started shaving once a day – or rather, Cecilia would shave me with the new straight razor she bought for us, as she seemed to take a fetishistic joy in the precarious role-play, especially when the blade met my throat.

On the third day in my new dwelling, it wasn't long before I was beginning to feel lost in her absence, even on her quick errand to buy groceries. My fog was suddenly burned away by the chime of her voice calling my name from outside, blanketing the pitter-patter of her heels up the cement steps. I swung open the door and ran outside like an excited, obedient captive.

"Can you help me with these bags? There are more in the car as well."

Hammocked in both her hands were plastic grocery bags, each bulging with two gallons of milk.

"Wowzers, lot of milk! You cooking or something?"

"Nooooooo…" she replied out of breath but still full of charm, "It's just this little thing I do."

I giggled, confused. I marched dutifully down the stairs to her car, ravenously starving, wondering what kinds of goodies she brought home that I could devour. I popped the trunk. To my further bemusement, there lay eight more shopping bags, each with the same two gallons of organic whole milk and one more with four liters of goat's milk. It was the most wholesome sick joke I had ever fallen victim to, though I still was not privy to the punch line. I grabbed them with a grin, cutting off my circulation quickly with two bags in each hand, swinging like wrecking balls. "Look at me!" I thought, "An instant milkmaid!" I ran up the stairs with this mysterious dairy-scale of justice, instead opting to feel tough, strong. A chivalrous provider!

After a quick two trips I reached the top and fell like a figurine, September's sweat feeling disgusting on my face as it absorbed into the carpet, its bristles intermingling with my stubble. I turned my head toward the staircase as Cecilia grabbed each gallon one by one and danced up the stairs like a ballerina. I thought I heard water running but was too tired to care. I laid there for an undetermined allotment but once I saw all the plastic bags empty and slowly swaying in noon's subtle breeze, a strange suspicion erected me.

After scaling the stairs I made sure to wipe off my mystified smirk. I made a right to the bathroom, the door already open. There she lay, enveloped in the nebulous murk of ivory-tinged heaven, nothing but her idol head exposed, eyes shut. An oozy smile of ecstasy slowly dripped over her, telling me that she knew I was there to witness her ritual milk bath. I had seen Jack throw himself crashing through a window and lick the blood from his wounds, laughing. I had seen the Bluesman drain every last drop from seven bottles of Night Train in less than three hours. I had seen us hot knife opium and smear it on our cigarettes. I had seen myself grabbing other people's cigarettes and putting them out on my own face before grabbing their drinks and emptying them into my boot and chugging from it just to shock them enough to leave my house, but never had I witnessed this particular brand of unapologetic decadence.

"Take off your clothes, please," she whispered, managing to sound like both a polite request and breathy demand.

Obliging to this baptism, the milky whiteness immediately rid me of any residual shyness. I immediately tangled myself up in her and felt the velvety results of her elegant weekly rite. Soon I could no longer tell what was flesh and what was milk. Once we were through, one third of the tub's cloudy contents was on the floor, as we lay there entangled and expired. She gracefully pulled the plug with her toes as we watched the rest go down the drain.

My head was hanging languid off the rim of the tub, her head on my stomach. A fluid passing of time almost lulled me to sleep before I noticed, out of the corner of my eye, something small and black dart out from the molding.

Then another.

And another.

Every time I would look over they seemed to disappear out of view. Whichever side I would try to lean my head to catch a glimpse, I failed to catch their actual definition in my scope. I dismissed these rascally black dots as those post-bath stars one gets when light-headed and has overstayed their welcome in steam leisure splendor. It was time to get out. I began to stir. Cecilia popped her head up out of the tub and promptly screamed.

"EEEEEEEEEEEAAAAAHHHHAAAHAHAHA!!!" her shriek trailing off into wholesome laughter, "awwwww... Look Caleb! They've followed you all the way to my home!"

I leaned over the tub, eyes slowly coming into focus. There stood three large cockroaches, antennas swaying in curiosity and strategically pointing in our direction, a perfect arrowhead constellation, starring right at us.

"What do you think they want from us?" she asked, a joke cloaked in genuine accusation.

"Well if you look at their antennas, you'll see they're pointed back. When they are resting, they point up and forward. So right now all we can say is that they are... No longer at rest."

It was only a month before Cecilia had a new proposition for me. She wanted to move.

"But I just got here…"

"I know," she defended, "but wouldn't it be great if we had a place that we could plant our flag and call our own? This place is too big for us and I can't keep it clean and there is still John Boy's ghosts of violence around every corner. I hate to put you through that kind of psychic torture…"

"Well, it's far from torture Cecilia, but if it would make you happy…"

"It would, it would! And I've already found a place!"

I tore the sideview mirror clean off as I parked another U-Haul in front of a cluster of bungalows which contained our new stream-lined abode. I had put us in reverse and clipped it hard against a wooden telephone pole, my inner dialogue was reminding me that I had come this far and not to look back. As I picked up the shattered mirror off the ground, I stood up face to face with a handmade flyer in Spanish for a missing teenager.

We were in Echo Park, and we were two unbeknownst locusts of a new generation slowly swarming in, gentrifying the area. Three un-amused Mexicans in white splattered painter's pants had barely finished the last touches renovating our unit as we began loading up the first batch of cardboard boxes. As we reached the top of the stairs, they filed out one by one without a sound as we tried to say hello.

Our new neighbors came out to greet us. There was Victor, a Latin Lavender Loverboy who emerged from his guests – a sun-bathing circle jerk – with a clenching smile that would immediately return to fill up the brief spaces after each word spoken. There was Robin, a bitter, reclusive lesbian that would barely open her mouth when faced with any obligatory pleasantries. And then there was Camille, a touchy-feely Coppertone vixen in her late 40s, always armed with her last glass of Chardonnay and a cigarette desperately needing to be ashed, if she could only stop talking for one second. She knew all the dirt about everyone on the property, and in L.A. in general. Those who she obviously didn't know, she made up stories about. She had lived on the property the longest and filled us in.

"Oh, so did the landlord tell you about your place, the previous tenants? There were three Mexican families living in the one-bedroom, and two other families lived in the basement. It wasn't up to code, so they just evicted them all without warning instead of fixing it up. Then they fixed it up and raised the rent and here you two are! So, welcome!" she said as she curtsied.

Our unit was on the highest point of the lot where the sun always seemed to be shining, at the top of winding cement stairs shoddily sculpted, boasting bohemian Spanish charm. We finished unloading and collapsed on the couch, deflated though proud to finally punctuate the day. We held each other smirking smugly, our eyes closed, the dog at our feet like a Norman Rockwell timeless vision of young lover utopia. We lay there until a new view of the moon arose above us, cueing us to open one of the two bottles of wine we had bought on the way there. I felt so immortal I drank one and a half of them and then went out for one more while Cecilia dozed off.

Upon returning I tried to wake her, maybe a little too rambunctiously as she responded with mumbles that quickly morphed into a bloody scream in full vibrato. Night terrors. She groggily begged me to leave her alone and that she would explain some other time. As she slipped back under, I popped open the cheap red and drank it out of the bottle as I stared out the window, humming an on the fly victory hymn. I paced back and forth the length of the living room, slaloming through half-opened boxes as my humming increased in volume. I remembered Camille mentioning the basement, and all of a sudden there was no place I would rather be, exploring every nook and cranny of our new domicile. I ran to the threshold and my shoulder clipped the doorjamb, spinning me to the floor. No one saw it so I remained on all fours unashamed, crawling down the stairs to the left of the house, where I had noticed a door. I raised myself to my knees and put my fingers into the hole where there was once a doorknob. I opened it just enough so I could crawl in, shutting it behind me to assure no light would interrupt my indulgence of complete darkness. My hands felt curious diagonal splintered wood surfaces and oblong plastic objects, bunches of plush fur I could cup in my palm, and then something I promptly tripped over. I lay there in what was sure to be a pure dirt floor comfortable enough to drift into my own drunken head and become invisible in the night, still humming…

Scalpels of sunlight did a cruel surgery on my eyes as Cecilia creaked open the basement door. It was 10:30am. I noticed that third bottle of wine in my hand as I lay on a broken door on the ground, surrounded by children's toys, rolling high chairs, car seats. It appeared I had used some bunched up moldy bedding as a pillow, all left behind from the evicted tenants. There she stood by the door, looking down at me with tears in her eyes.

"Cecilia, I am so sorry. I'm not sure what happened…"

Her head down in her hands, she began to sob.

"Cecilia, please! Everything's ok… I was just excited and kept drinking and every once in a while…"

"Caleb…" she spoke as if she was drowning, "you have to come upstairs and see this. It's horrible."

"Look!"

She pointed at the wall in the living room, still crying. It was the only electrical socket in the room, in a bizarre corner light-years away from any logical place you would put a modern day appliance. She had gotten up early and already arranged all our larger luxuries in some bastardized version of feng shui and this was clearly nuisance enough to make her meltdown.

"This means we're going to have to get an extension cord and it's going to make the whole house look like absolute stray noodle SHIT!!" Her foot stomped with the four-letter word.

"Shhhhhhh…. shhhhhh… shush, shush, shush," I took her by the shoulders and held her, "listen, I'll take care of it. Be right back!"

I returned a half hour later after running red lights to the Hollywood Home Depot and back. I had bought a twenty-five-foot extension cord, which for some reason was only available in carnation yellow, so I bought some opaque white electrical tape that matched the paint to sweeten my handy plan. I ran the yellow cord along the edge of the floor all the way to the estranged socket, then meticulously cut the tape so it wouldn't create any unsightly creases, before I laid it along the whole length of the cord with one continuous slide of my thumb. It looked immaculately like part of the molding as I stood up with my hands on my hips, satisfied for saving the day. Cecilia walked in, having just changed into a turquoise sundress. She looked down at my handy work, her eyes following it all the way to the power strip where she saw the cord's exposed yellow head plugged in. She began, again, to cry.

"YELLOW?!?! YELLOW!!! What are you trying to tell me Caleb?"

I fell to the couch, in silence and utter confusion.

"Caleb!!! Everyone knows carnation yellow represents rejection! Distain! Disappointment!!!" she screamed as she counted them off her fingers, "now look who's disappointed!! IT'S ALL WRONG!!!"

She fell to her knees, covering her dripping eyes with balled fists that were no muzzle for the hysteria bellowing out.

"It's all wrong... All wrong."

As her dissolving voice echoed through the living room, I could only remain quiet, as if something had robbed me of my own. I had curled up into a fetal position on the couch, holding my gut as I felt the most unbearable burning inside my abdomen. My will began to shut down and I felt my limbs go numb. At that very moment I felt a loss of will to move ever again.

NINE

"Once the Emerald Wasp has steered the roach to its burrow, she then lays a 2mm long white egg on the roach's abdomen. As it's now time to exit, the wasp covers the hole of the burrow with pebbles for extra insurance to keep would-be predators out."

“ I am nesting..."

She finally broke the abysmal silence with this cliffhanger of intent. She looked at me with grave, determined eyes to explain, but not necessarily to apologize, "this is just what we do, Caleb. Young couples naturally want to create an atmosphere in their homes to feel safe, sensible. Everything has its place and aesthetic to reflect our identities, which are nothing more than our desires."

I was listening to her lesson of domestic bliss lying down, as my stomach still panged. It was slightly, though not altogether, similar to the ulcers I would get as a teen and with every passing minute it actually felt world's apart – distinct with the thick sensation of a venomous adrenaline coursing through my veins in rhythm with the ache in my belly. She paced back and forth with her arms outstretched to nothing as she spoke, wearing her new turquoise pantsuit cinched with a gold belt. I was beginning to notice her peculiar shift in taste, this being the third teal outfit in the last three days, all of which were adorned with shiny gold accessories – that gold lamé belt, bracelets and new age medallions around her neck. As she continued to speak, her words had a wrecking ball weight that slowly swung me up and out the door.

"Ok," I exhaled, "I'm going for a walk…" even though I knew the bar was just a block away – you just don't ever find yourself saying "I am going for a beeline." I knew what would make this abdominal pain go away, or at least temporarily make me forget about it. I would drink anything in the bar's arsenal that at the least would trade today's arrival of unholy pain for tomorrow's hell-bound hangover. Walking to the bar, I felt as though I had just been poisoned, and the only rational solution would be to willfully poison myself in order to reverse the direction of her intent. Ultimately, I wanted to not just overpower, but actually *become* poison – to drink as means of protest, akin to a Tibetan monk lighting himself on fire.

It was just past five, happy hour – in Los Angeles this meant an almost empty bar thanks to the mass defeat of rush hour traffic. I felt cradled in the darkness as the door swung shut behind me. I had been coming to this place – formerly a veteran cop haunt – the last three days in a row. Joe the bartender already knew my usual. He looked to his left, smiled, nodded and began fixing my first of seven boilermakers that night, as I eventually achieved the dizzying heights of the many tiers of poison. The bellyache and I successfully dissolved into the shadows of the bar and my mind.

I awoke the next day on the couch and immediately knew it was my doghouse. I had blacked out and traded my stomach pain for a splitting migraine that didn't so much ache as it burned and throbbed in rhythm of my heartbeat, which was slow but had the deep resonance of a tympani. I felt powerless, not knowing where she was, not knowing what time it was, not knowing what day it was, not being able to move except for my hands squeezing my head, as if it would help. My mind began doing donuts in slippery cul-de-sacs. *Ever since I moved in with her, she seems to think I'm straight out of "The Lost Weekend" or "Days of Wine and Roses,"* I thought, *Almost as if she wants it, willing it to be true... Where's my trench coat, I know she's always hated that thing... Has she left me? I meant no harm, just wanted to disappear for a bit...*

I noticed my pants were not only unbuttoned, but my cock was out. Not only was my cock out, but there was some slimy residue around the head. *Oh fuck, was I jerking off out here?!?* I panicked at the thought of me coming home, forgetting where I was, who I was living with and making myself fucking comfy?!?! I wanted to die right there and then.

But something worse happened – the front door opened and Cecilia walked in, somehow smiling, though I believe I turned over to hide my slimy spent dick just in time.

"Rise and shine! I got you a little something..."

I was absolutely horrified. Was this a trick?

"I couldn't bear to see you in that thing anymore so I took it upon myself to get you a new one!"

She held up a new grey hounds tooth trench coat. It was a nice, thoughtful gesture, if not for the resentment I had regarding the whereabouts of my old beloved one - so many smells, memories, and my own self ground into its adventurously fraying fibers. My stomach churned again.

"Shucks, Cece, that's amazing. Now I've got two..."

"Well, no. You don't. I got rid of the other one." she said.

"What do you mean you got *rid*?"

"I buried it out back. Don't worry, you'll never find it."

"Cecilia!!! That was my jacket!!! You had no right to do that. It was my second skin!"

"I wanted to do something nice for you. After last night..."

Slow, strange and full of wide-eyed innocence she recounted the evening with a certain rehearsed pride, realizing my lack of recollection. According to her, she finally went out looking for me and found me at the bar around 10:45pm, a time where I knew my view had to have already turned dark sepia. She sat down next to me without a word and ordered a vodka cranberry. I was so amorous that I threw my arms around her instantly. She pushed me away and threw her drink in my face and began tearing me apart with words she claimed were even upsetting the bartender. I fired back with whatever I had until the bickering reached a fever pitch, then knocked my own drink off the bar to give myself room to get up and stand up on the thing. Once I got my balance I pointed straight down at her and proclaimed, "You know why I drink like this?!? Because you make me feel IMMORTAL!!!"

Supposedly there was some applause from the bar. The bartender was laughing at this point as he helped me down. We had a couple more rounds. One on the house. We went home around midnight and she fucked me. I was relieved it was genuine sex and not me being a deviant in her new house of the holy, so relieved in fact I forgot all about my maudlin coat that was now worm food. It was time for another walk.

"Uh, no. None of that really happened. Well, okay maybe half of it but there wasn't any real cinematic ending like she's making it sound. It was... sad. Just kind of sad."

Joe the bartender gave me the uncut lowdown after I came in there apologizing profusely for making any kind of scene the night before. "Man, you were fine!" he said, "She came in here like a fucking demon and started screaming at you and dragged you out by your lapels. Maybe you drank yourself a little limp but mainly you just seemed a little too embarrassed to resist. Everyone that saw couldn't stop talking about how bad they felt for you."

I put my head down into my crossed arms.

"Oh and she did throw a drink in your face, but she grabbed it right out from the hands of one of our regulars."

My head and stomach began to pound with such a force that all I could do was start clawing at myself. Joe asked if I was okay.

"You need anything?"

"Yes, give me two. One to occupy each of these," I said as I held up my hands, "because you know, idle hands…"

I took them both to the farthest dark corner, downed them both, and resumed my head in my clasped arms. Pain, bewilderment, exhaustion, and then some kind of second cousin far-removed from actual sleep.

I floated back to our bungalow, slowly walking the cement path to our steps, though it was as if the cement was freshly laid, both thick and wet enough to slow my pace to a taunting degree. All lights were off, but something inside illuminated the walls enough to see a silhouette of what could only be Cecilia, walking past, stopping at the front window. She turned to face my direction, though these shadows were unkind to the face I loved, causing her head to take on a grotesque shape with what looked like antennas sprouting out of the top. These shadows did not dance or alter, and my stomach clenched when her image came into view. The shiny, scaly head of an insectoid had taken the place of her gorgeous human one and it was clearly not a mask. She was a wasp. I was not surprised. I was not afraid. Instead I felt possessed by her presence, frozen and taken in by her cold shadow. The brilliant green luminescence from her new form stopped at the bottom of her neck and blurred seamlessly into her human flesh where she was stark naked right down to her still kissable toes, her genitalia intact as I left it, her breasts still retained their firm, perky presence... But her eyes!!! Her eyes that I thought were big and beautiful before now took up each side of her face and shone smooth and opaque like obsidian. Momentarily hypnotized, I saw my reflection in them like that day when I looked into the box office window, which housed all the initial incantations of this curse. We had come full circle. She was waiting for me. Everything finally revealed, though she did not say a word. I had never been so paralyzed with fear and attraction in my life. I could not stop walking towards the front door to face my true love, my version of union and sacrifice.

We were not alone. As I advanced, she walked in reverse to reveal the company. Illuminated from the religious votive candles that lined the floor, the shadows flickered and danced but the men did not move, remaining at solemn attention with their backs against the wall - these living, breathing men who it seemed were taking the roles of mere inanimate columns, surrounding and containing the impending ritual. A non-descript bed that looked more like a carefully dressed massage table stood in the middle of the room. Decorative tapestry adorned the walls where they were once white. I did not question the mystery of any of this unfolding before me, despite the men appearing so independently obedient as if they were each holding a pistol to their own heads.

Cecilia backed up to the center of the room, arms outstretched in presentation.

"I have chosen you." she said, confidently grave.

With that, a slight but collective rustle from the men as they poised themselves for what was to happen next. Some looked deflated as much as the others appeared anxious, they could barely hold still.

As if there had been a dress rehearsal, I approached the bed, my movements synchronized with her motioning that direction. I slowly threw a leg over and got horizontal. Cecilia approached and began to remove my pants before unbuttoning my shirt with surgical precision. Wasting no time as she let the shirt tail fall from my abdomen, she clasped both hands around my cock and began to manually arouse me, ignoring the fact that the mere sight of her naked body had already worked its inherent magic on my pulsing, blood engorged tool – wasp or no wasp. By the sound of my first uncontrolled exhalation, she decided it was time. Gracefully, she placed one knee after the other onto the table, positioning herself in a squat that hovered just inches from my cock, still in her firm grip. She was so close I could feel the gentle tease of her pubic hair sweeping across the head, and when I couldn't hold still any longer, she slowly descended on me. I felt the thin ribbons of her threshold surround me before the head plunged fully into her, the slow slide of the inevitable fusing us both together as close as one man and one vixen insectoid could possibly be.

She gyrated in fluid, churning circles as I felt her walls moisten further. Her nether region devoured me with every hungry thrust. My head whipped to the right, then left, then right again, when I saw the men's solemn mood turn to lurching interest. They all seemed present with a sense of impending purpose, and we had all reached this understanding beyond the use of words, though there was the looping, haunting mantras somehow broadcast into my head that I knew they could all hear as well... *Nether Region! Liebestod!! La Petite Morte!* Intertwining into this buzzing telephone line of pure mortal coil, taking the place of my brain like a hollow cavern. As she continued to thrash my cock inside of her like a haywire garbage disposal, it dawned on me that this cerebral switcharoo was the origin of my splitting headache. I thrust into her as hard as I could once I realized I had lived in ignorance of this psychic lobotomy. She stabbed herself into me rapidly in retaliation, like a wound pushing itself back into the knife. I moaned to a God I did not believe in with primitive ecstasy, as I felt a shudder and warmth rush through my groin. Cecilia took notice of my impending climax and met me half way, as she shrieked the bloodiest sound I have ever tried plugging my ears to. But two of the men had already rushed over to hold my arms down. There she screamed, arms outstretched reaching for the rest of the men from the walls, as they all stepped forward on cue, surrounding the table and grabbing Cecilia's shoulders, giving hard gravity to hold her in place, as I exploded into her and her into me. Her ritual complete.

A burst of sharp pain followed by numbness blossomed into my lips amidst a commotion that seemed miles above an ocean's surface. By the third bludgeon it had regained its full volume of machismo panic, like men hollering as they wrestle down an alligator. Her cries drowned them out, confusing the aim and intent as their fists made perfect contact with my face.

"Hold him down!"

I awoke to a living nightmare, again, not knowing how I got there. I was on *her* bed being held down by two of Cecilia's male friends as the larger curly haired brute took repeated swings at my face. I could only twist and thrash in their grasp, while using my legs to kick them off. In the middle of the struggle my foot accidentally connected with Cecilia, causing her to fly off the bed onto the floor; making my mere shizoid blacked-out bumblings graduate into a skewed version of domestic violence to a cocktail-attired lynch mob that was already doling out their punishment on me.

Through a stinging veil of blood and sweat I saw her leaning against the leg of the bed, crying in confused hysterics. She no longer had the head of a wasp like she had in the *dream*, one I swore was as real as the beating I was in the middle of. Her dinner guests finished me off, and before long I was dragged out of our house and left on the lawn.

"He's drunk again!" she screamed to her guests as I walked in the door that night, as if my mere unconscious presence was somehow equivalent to raising my fist at her. She raised the bar of this framed charade by running into her room to hide, her spiraling cries barely muffled through her slammed door. This instantly raised a thick demonized suspicion to her three guests, all men that had decided long ago they didn't care for me.

"What have you been doing to her?!" the tall one interrogated.

Instead of answering, I stumbled into the kitchen and grabbed a bottle of red on the counter and one of those metal corkscrews – the kind with the little arms that raise up as it digs into the cork. I stabbed the bottle with it and quickly gave up, too obliterated and adrenaline-blind to focus. There was another one of these corkscrews on the stove so I grabbed that one as well, now armed with one in each hand.

"What the fuck have you been doing to her, Caleb?!" the tall one repeated, his two friends in tow, as they entered the kitchen to corner me.

Choosing the high road, I said nothing at all as I communicated through pantomime. I became possessed by the corkscrews. Eyes closed and hands to my side, I slowly raised them up like an archangel boasting his wings, mimicking the corkscrew's almost comedic triumph of function, as if the inanimate gadget declares, "Horray!" once the screw penetrates to its deepest reaches. I held both my arms above my head in prideful surrender, though armed with potential weapons, the boys naturally took it as a coax as I played the role of a blind matador. The tall one lunged and socked me right in the cheek, as the others grabbed me out of the kitchen, pulling me into the living room where my pantomime turned into some kind of interpretive dance that could have made a whirling dervish bow out. The tall one grabbed me by the neck. The two others coerced Cecilia out of our bedroom and threw me on the bed. All three of them held me down, assuming they could tell a zombie to "go to sleep." Don't ever attempt to wake or tell a dipso-somnambulist to go to bed, as they reside in the realm of the over-lapping in-between, where there are no rules; there is no telling what they can and will do to shake up your shared reality if coun-teracted with anything other than their own stream of instinct! I fought against the weight of these hands holding me down, kicking, screaming, thrashing - having futuristic flashbacks of the loony bins I was doomed for. *They are finally here to take me away* was all I could think as I wiggled, growling as I convulsed out of their claws, finally activating their windmill of fists.

All of the attention on me! When could I take my bow? To be dragged out of my own house by strangers as a result of an intric-ately orchestrated domestic abuse fraud from unknown motives! I had developed an emotional emphysema from a union tempered by fire, smoke, and mirrors. When one thinks of all the disgustingly placid and superficial paths of love people skip merrily down, it is our first instinct to assume these idiots are shallow and this is all they have ever known and therefore all they are able to handle. On the contrary, there is a great chance these moronic displays of empty congruence are formed from these trials by flame I was now experi-encing - a way to keep further trauma at bay, for as long as they could stand to be a shadow of their former selves. This happiness that is formed from a pre-mature senility, the PTSD after the war portion of love – one could only hope for this. As I lay on the lawn, my backside damp with dew, blood and saliva forming quaint mini-ature landscapes of trickling rivers from my swollen lips; as I inhaled the fresh air of evening about to become a cruel dawn, I felt the wheeze of this emphysema and traced it directly to my heart, both the cause and effect. I was being suffocated by dread now, that there was something permanent in the corner of our bedroom, beyond her lame fawn collapse. Our third mind had been conjured, and was now towering over both of us. We had been indoctrinated, though further confused by this baptism beyond the buoy in the ocean of another larger presence. The wasp and the cockroach as these totems, overlapping to create the in-between, where there is no absolute darkness and no definitive light. Where only the utmost sinister kinks of nature can be nourished by the stubborn existence of two people trying to insist that they are one, alone.

Two days later I received a call from my Mother.

"So! I am almost done with these patterns for the costumes…" she gleefully started before she inquired about my measurements.

"Costumes?" I asked, having no idea what she was planning. I realized it was half way through October.

"Well, yeah? You don't know about this? I figured it was your idea…"

They had been talking. Not about my alleged crimes, not stoking the drama of young adult love seeing its expiration date as a light shining through a darkening tunnel.

With the knowledge that my Mother worked as a costume tailor at the local playhouse, Cecilia had gone to her with some Halloween plans she either wanted to surprise me with, or just go ahead and pass the point of no return, to reduce the chance of me intervening - often one and the same motive. Annoyed, I rattled off some numbers of how small I felt at that particular moment, and hung up.

Cecilia was in the kitchen nook, writing down some festive pumpkin-kissed recipe out of an Autumn cookbook. Almost forty-eight hours had passed since *The Night of Bottomless Infamy* and I had done everything in my power to make good. I was that beaten down. I was convinced I was the most evil man alive. I even begged for the phone numbers of her dinner guests so I could apologize, but she insisted that it would do more damage. She made this scenario airtight, in a panic to change the subject. I saw even more darkness through these occasional holes in the fog, and it was clear she was hiding something, just heavy enough to carry without dropping.

"Who was on the phone?" she asked, sing-songy.

"It was my Mother. What are these costumes?"

She threw her head back and laughed, just as she did in the Kibbitz Room where we were all made privy to a murder.

"Ahhhhh... Damn! That was supposed to be a surprise. I thought I told her not to tell you. What did she tell you?"

"Not much. Caught me off guard. She asked for my measurements and I hung up. I didn't think to ask questions..."

"Good."

"Because my head still hurts."

What exactly synchronized my pain, fatigue and loss of will with her sharpened denial and stabbing persistence, I would never know.

TEN

"For the next three days, the roach will simply sit paralyzed while the egg slowly hatches. Once the larvae is hatched, it feeds on the roach for nourishment for another four to five days before finally eating its way into the roach's abdomen where the larvae proceeds to live as an endoparasitoid. For the following eight days, the larvae will consume the roach's internal organs but only in a specific order which will maximize the likelihood of the roach staying alive. This is until the larvae enters its pupal stage and forms a cocoon inside the roach's body, eventually causing the roach to explode once the fully grown wasp unfurls itself to emerge and flaps its new wings. Development is faster, with higher level of success during the warm season."

Fall had finally cooled the hot coal of the streets – like a sprawling multi-circuit River Styx, this change of temperature made it that much more intimidating to cross over. A sudden cool breeze can trigger the fear that there is something else in control of our respective fates. It was October 30th, a Friday night, and all the elements were in place to make a lost weekend out of Halloween, rain or shine.

She made plans for us on what is affectionately known in some cities as Devil's Night, a holiday designated for arson made popular in Detroit. But Los Angeles is so psychic-level combustible we have to designate a whole measure of time to sporadic infernos – August to New Year's is Fire Season – spanning three of the four seasons that the rest of the world observes. We found ourselves smack in the middle of this with no conceivable exit but to keep walking the embers, as we passed the point of no return.

We were to have some drinks with her friends and see where the night went from there. I had stopped trying to mix my circle of pals with hers a long time ago – it was a kindling of cattiness and misunderstanding, each side growing up planets apart, not speaking a similar language, right down to simple facial expressions.

I punctuated this imbalance by assuming my stonewall face for the evening, try as they might to disassemble me. It was not rebellion I strove for, but a willful, walking Passion Play, tailor-made for the discerning public eye; that could only gawk silently with their own psychic sympathies. "What in the world happened to that poor man?" I projected in reverse to the oncoming nightlife – that formless chattering entity that these days gave me equal parts ostracism and paranoia, as I was no longer part of its cast – meaning both its allegiance and its boasting shadows. As we walked out the door I noticed a bulging white trash bag, barely containing some kind of Earth-toned plush fabric that I could only assume were the forsaken costumes. I yanked the bag up by a tear that had already started in its skin, now thin and transparent after being pushed to its furthest limits, not unlike my own. In a split second she grabbed my hand away, scolding. Uncanny. She had been walking two steps ahead of me. This I was clearly unable to explain away by some hyper-acute woman's intuition, but like eyes in the back... No! On the top of her head, as she was in the middle of throwing her head back, laughing to herself again. Wasn't she?

We arrived at a cacophonic Mexican restaurant, where the only Mexicans in attendance were the one's serving us. "Margs!" Cecilia and her friends proclaimed like divinity the fifth time we asked what we were going to do. "We're in the mood for Margs!" I had sensed a nameless, oncoming dread of the evening before we left. Now in the thick of it I felt that at any moment I could step up to the plate to wholeheartedly contribute to its source.

After being showed to our table I ordered two *Margs*, one for each clenched fist, referring to them by that exact moronic abbreviation as I glared daggers at the rest of the table, who at this point would be deer in the dark - before whiplashing my head to Cecilia to ask what she wanted to drink. She froze after realizing one was not for her.

"Uhm, just a Margertia please!" she nervously told the waiter, "No, wait! No. Two please!" she corrected her order as she gave me a sideways checkmate glance, a vain attempt to be neck and neck with my dreaded audacity.

So it continued, clockwise around the table of six, two *Margs* for each victim of a phantom peer pressure I started as a means of accelerated numbing or heavy artillery, which ever came first. The overlapping small talk of inside jokes I was not privy to had barely started, when the waiter arrived with a dozen sickly sweet aquariums, full of what looked like piss after vitamins, almost overflowing over the rim caked with gravel-sized salt. Sweet. Salty. Company unsavory.

This sad hybrid of infectious emotional runoff had changed the chemical make-up of Caleb's blood, as it slowly began to both thin and thicken like some time-released quantum glitch, rendering his motor skills useless, and now he no longer had a voice, much less a memory, therefore he can't really tell the rest of this story from his perspective. He is numb from head to toe, and it is hard to tell whether this is a reaction of our "love chemicals" or a bodily defense from Post Traumatic Stress Disorder. He can move slightly, but it's pathetically akin to a mentally disabled Praying Mantis, or as we have found, a cockroach in the throes of being stung by an Emerald Wasp.

The dual toxins were now wholly conjoined – her unholy secretions/psychic napalm infused in his unquenchable lust for drink, which in his mind was the antidote to any further downward suction – his determined dulling of emotion a result of personal emergency. As it turns out, she wanted the same outcome, only with different motives and ways of achieving it. She required him as a vessel – though he could have been anyone - something she could hollow out, as well as someone that could act as – or be reduced to – a two-dimensional decoy for the rest of the world to rest assured that another young couple was in love and would lead by example, for the species to continue to procreate and consume – in her own species' world it was one and the same act.

Mood: Tense, ostracizing, ricocheting private jokes Caleb is not privy to. Classic drunken paranoia where one misunderstands every word for a tailor-made curse. A brittle, noisy Cassevettes scene, where every time there is a pause in dialogue it's quickly made up for with for with multiple voices talking over each other. Caleb is uncomfortably quiet at first, but with every sip it seems to open pores of cock-brow delinquent malevolence, a diarrhea-slurping grin. His rapid imbibing starts as a means to numb himself from the inherent isolation that comes from not mixing well with company, and the headache he is being administered from the chatter. They had known each other since junior high and somehow still acted that immature. The air, thick with ambiguously taunting cackling from the men and women alike – serendipitously dressed up like witches and warlocks for the impending holiday. Caleb, for the first time he can remember, or not recall at all, is not going out of his way to make good around this insufferable company, who spent most of their upbringings in Malibu trashing their wealthy families vacation homes when they didn't get their way. In fact, he is double fisting "MARGS" as the rest of the table refers to them when ordering from the unimpressed waiter. Caleb too, begins ordering them by this idi-

otic abbreviation – though not to save time in a celebratory manner... Every time he orders, now six deep, he pans the rest of the
table slow enough to catch each one of them in his blinding head-
lights in order to let them know just how vapid they come across.
"MARGS!" is all he says in creepy crawling faux-solidarity, scanning
the table slow with a suspicious prison guard stare.

Approximately an hour has passed when they are finally ready
to order, waiter present but mentally checked-out after coming back
for the fifth time to ask if they are ready to eat. Everyone at the table
orders elaborate combination plates. Caleb is the last to order. All
eyes on him. Silence.

"And sir? What would you like?"

"I would like a beer. Two beers."

"Aren't you eating?" Cecilia asks, mortified in half-whisper.

"Yes. Liquid bread..."

Two Coronas arrive immediately, but the waiter leaves with a
weary glance over the shoulder to Caleb, who has already drained
half a bottle in two aggressive swills.

"Caleb!"

"Hey! Lissen!!! There's a lotta big rocky salts on those MARGS!
I'm fugging dehydrated, ok?"

Twenty minutes later dinner arrives. "Hot plate coming! Careful
please," says the waiter, almost to warn them of something other
than the food. The party nervously digs into their meals, mournfully
squirming as Caleb watches them all like a hawk and laughs, though
there are no jokes now, inside or otherwise. He spends equal time
with each person, staring at them. Watching their every bite. Their
heads down because they can feel his eyes – they watch in bemused
horror as he does the same to each. They concentrate on their food,
not because they're necessarily hungry, but as means to distract, es-

cape, a vain diffusion. But there he was, every time they would get the guts to look up to start some desperate conversation, there he was staring, grinning, drooling, glazed, entranced like a orphan that hadn't had a meal in days, looking through the window, doubling as the Horseman of Famine. He starts to drool voluntarily from the corner of his mouth for shock histrionics but now he just can't stop. They might as well have been on the bus where the only empty seat was one next to the odiferous schizo, no where to turn but strangers curious eyes and the jarring clank of glasses, plates, all sounding like brief but frequent shatterings of their general safety and self-confidence. The racket seemed to ricochet erratic and un-playful around the crowded interior, spraying out of every tight angle or wide occupied space. We see Caleb's attention darting to and fro, to anywhere now but the table, trying to capture every shrill scrape and rim hit, then mimicking with his own unruliness at the table, which was growing more intolerable by the second. The rest of the group had long run out of clever buffer to ignore his unsightly transgressions. He senses their discomfort and somehow instantly forgets that it was all decidedly malicious on his part, quickly turns self-conscious by their solemn, shameful expressions, their hands now shielding their eyes, squinting as if they were staring into the sun. The vicious cycle now half-way through: euphoria, confusion, self-consciousness, displaced anger. We hear Caleb mumble something, see him grab an unfinished MARG, throwing it back with abandon before getting up to leave without announcement. But no declaration is necessary as he falls backwards into their waiter full of another round for the table, tray and drinks crashing on top of their server and Caleb, now overlapped in a crucifix of sad, splayed humanity.

In the melee, Caleb had grabbed onto whatever he could to break his fall, which happened to be the slack from the thick white table cloth, three dimpled crimson candle holders overturn on the plush material, setting it instantly aflame and assuring their own unintentional but pre-determined Devil's Night in front of an audience of gawking, formless witnesses.

Pairs of Penny-loafers start stomping on the burning tablecloth, half-off the aborted banquet. Damp soiled rags and origami napkins quickly unravel and are swung in an arched hammering motion, whipping at the flame like the accelerating foreplay of a locker room gang-bang.

We see waiters screaming at Cecilia, and her whole faint-hearted jittery litter to get him the hell out or they're calling the cops. Almost boasting an unprecedented hollowness, their instinct is just to abandon him to the elements, where we have so far seen: Santa Ana winds, half-empty spilled glasses of water, accidental arson, and later, Earth. Instead, the tall one grabs him and throws him over his shoulder, the rest in embarrassed, face-covered tow. American Express is swiped, and they tip a paltry 5%, so frantic to leave they don't look at the total and had long lost track of "MARGS."

In the car now, Caleb sprawled in the very back of Cecilia's Sport Utility Vehicle. The occupants are so drunk they are now laughing at the absurdity of the mess they curiously now try to take credit for from a safe distance but it is far from lighthearted as they rub Caleb's name in the mud in the same breath, he who is only semiconscious and moaning. The collective embarrassment has quickly gone from mortified to cruel comedy, poking fun at the Mexican workers having to clean up after the yuppies-in-training and whether they should find the nearest vacant lot to ditch him. They ask out loud what she is still doing with him and she replies that she is not done with him quite yet, but soon.

There were some flashes of what you wouldn't dare call clarity – to even call him awake, one would probably pull a muscle – but some vague, liquid moments where his eyes were actually able to focus on his surroundings. He could tell he was on her couch, that it was somehow daytime, but didn't know where the night went, and

before he could embrace any disconcertion, he was being assisted
lifting the glass to his lips so he wouldn't keep spilling all over himself, in which he quickly forgot where he was and had to ask again,
his own home becoming foreign, lacking substance and history.
Somehow, the garishness of the cockroach costume he found himself
trapped in, made in secrecy by his own Mother with all its
cumbersome extensions, was the least of his worries. In fact, he just
kept giggling, when he wasn't asleep, drooling...

Acceptance.

(He was dreaming that he was in the middle of a rolling dune
desert, on a crude obstacle course made solely of used tires laid out
in tandem pairs, this pattern continued as far as the eye could see, a
reinforced rubber chain who's only purpose seemed to be assuring
that the sadistic path was real and not just a man seeing double. He
lifted one leg up and over one at a time, steady as he goes, out of
one hole and into another, bringing each knee closer to his chin with
every hoist, as this scenario also boasted the feature of that old children's board game where if you touched the inside rim, you'd get an
alarming buzz; so leverage and height were key to make each step
successful. Although the length of this path was undetermined – not
just ahead of him, but behind him – Caleb wondered what was
making each simple step feel like he was wearing cinder block
sneakers; as every time he lifted his leg he felt gravity pull it square
into the dull rubber of each tire ahead of him, giving him a quick
but uncomfortable full-body shock, each one taking another ounce
of strength from his endurance. The reason revealed itself with
laughter, as he looked down to a non-descript bald-headed man in a
sweat suit with both hands on Caleb's ankles, trying to direct each
leg into the tire ahead. It was clear that this uninvited "coach" was
doing more harm than good, and with every electrocution from the

rims, he would berate and insult Caleb, followed by laughter at the absurdity of his lack of skill, despite the fact that his clumsiness was due to the overzealous weight of the man's pudgy hands.)

Soon always arrives sooner than you think when you are not waiting for it, or when you're so full of poison that you have indeed become poison - when one's eyes have rolled into the back of their head, you are not looking at the clock. For better or worse, as if the choice of the two extremes might soften what is really happening, the car has come to an abrupt halt, and Caleb stirs slightly.

He had lost a full day. It was now Halloween night, and their arrival to a party Caleb wouldn't typically want to attend was not disputed by his nearly unconscious mind, nor his lame limbs, as they got him out of the car pulling one ankle at a time, Cecilia running around the other side of the back seat to push the rest of him out onto his feet that would feel like they were staked into the ground, that is, if Caleb could feel anything right now besides the unfeeling of his astral oblivion. They propped him up like a scarecrow and foolishly expected this effigy to begin walking. He fell forward like lumber, no attempt to break his own fall as his head joined the concrete with a sound not unlike a pumpkin thrown against a similar unforgiving surface. But out of Caleb's head flowed steady streams of blood down his face, not seed and slime - that was to be found inside the party.

Without sympathy, they argued what to do with him.

"I am NOT missing this party. Fuck this!"

"Let's just bring him through the back and sit him down and pretend like we found him on the lawn? That way he'll be their responsibility?" someone whispered in insecure up-speak, where every statement is delivered as a question.

It was unanimous for all that were still conscious. Simply leaving him there like an empty bottle, Cecilia led the group into the house, looking back every couple steps to make sure he wasn't moving, and wasn't about to follow them. Once they were swallowed by the celebration and out of sight, he did begin to move, each limb one by one traveling upward towards the air as he remained on his back. His legs like a cyclist, peddling, as in his mind he saw himself walking. His arms reached out for her in vain as if he was shadowing her, but the vastness of the night sky remained an opaque veil of unresolved wonder. Who was this human cockroach, doing this Raid-sprayed pantomime, moving through the death-throes of dignity?

He turned over, limbs falling to the ground as he curled up into pill-bug protection, throwing his arms over and past his face into a prayer to nothing, almost mimicking the crescent moon above him. He opened his eyes just enough to see the house slowly spinning, then retracting, like a broken film reel about to burn. In a fluid motion not unlike one of a worm finding its composure after a harsh rain, Caleb brought his fingers to his eyes to pry them all the way open, to focus on his path as his stomach began to churn and deteriorate its own inner reaches, which gave him the will to rise, to make his grand entrance.

He put both hands on his knee and made it stand, bringing half of his body with him. Putting the other foot down, he was up, reanimated by adrenaline from the battlefield of his stomach and his glowing hatred, no longer displaced. Angry like a train, slowly chug-a-chugging toward the light of this invasively lit tunnel, out of the vacuum of night he approached the steps of the front porch where party-goers in limbo merely took up space and created more obstacles in his true path, all feeling the need to comment on his progress and speech with giggling inquiries, as if he were the appetizer to the night's main course.

"What the fuck is he saying?" someone wondered, "He keeps saying something over and over…"

Whipping his head to the left of the loudest offender, Caleb grabbed him by his shitty scarf.

"I AM RETURNING!!!"

"Duuuuude! You just got here!" the scarf-sporter said as everyone else laughed along.

And with that Caleb threw his arms back in perfect crucifix, the theme of the weak/week, heave-hoing a steady but wild stream of neon yellow projectile vomit all over the steps, splashing onto various sockless ankles in dress shoes, making everyone instantly rise to their feet.

"I AM RETURNING!!!" he said for all those who's attention he had finally demanded. There were hands trying to touch him to lead him away, outnumbered by all the other hands holding their eyes and noses.

Caleb at the threshold, he scans the room as everyone stops what they're doing, bit by the bug of the commotion outside, the mob forming.

He zeros on Cecilia, who is halfway down the hall waiting for the bathroom, too enthralled with admiring a boy's face make-up who had bastardized the re-appropriation of Dia de Los Muertos.

"I AM RETURNING!!!" he screamed, this time undeniably in her direction. Her large eyes darted toward him, her hand falling from the face of the painted boy, who looked as frightened as a skeleton could be – not so much by the non-sequitur he was howling at them, but at the six of his friends that were trying to grab onto Caleb as he repeatedly managed to successfully to fight each one off.

Now three feet away, he throws all his weight in a lunge toward her, bringing her crashing to the ground with him. Most onlookers too shocked and chickenshit to completely intervene, save all their hands screwing with his face, as he still tried to gasp out,

"I AM RETURNING..."

He knew she never wore underwear so he knew he could do it all in a flash. He spread open her legs as he did many times before out of loving tribute to her, but this time it held a deeper sanctity of emergency.

Throwing his head down into a quick ceremonious nod, he vomited more glowing bile right into her crotch, as she screamed and squirmed in hysterics, as if she had a fighting chance to escape what was already covering her... Everyone reached to intervene but instead only got covered in his sacred sick.

"...YOUR SEED!!!"

Cecilia managed a square kick to his face as the bumbling swarm grabbed him by his ankles and pulled him across the cluttered floor, wrinkling the Persian carpet and taking the corner of it with him, as he remained gurgling a trail of vomit that led to and from her smothered flower. He knew they had dragged him outside when the night air hit his face along with the smack of each concrete stair. The mob's frantic chatter was invasive to the serenity he now felt, even as the sirens drew closer. As they threw him on the moist, cold lawn all he could do was stare at the night sky, and there it was – the Milky Way, smeared across the heavens like discarded jism, dodging the bullet, the penetrating sting of impregnation, of a new life, unwanted, unwarranted.

THE
INTRUSION

SYMPTOMS OF ALCOHOLIC BLACKOUT & METAPHYSICAL HANGOVER

1. Negative emotional or physical reactions to the idea of spiritual detox (*part* of you wanting it, the other *part* of you not wanting it).
2. Physical, emotional, mental, and spiritual senses feeling "blocked."
3. You drank. You did drugs.
4. Sudden compulsive desires.
5. Inexplicable perspiration.
6. Sensing an unexplainable presence in your home, especially while falling asleep or when waking up in the middle of the night.
7. Insomnia.
8. Sudden and mysterious strife and conflict with loved ones.
9. Nausea and vomiting.
10. Addiction to sex.
11. Sudden onset of sadness, depression.
12. Reckless behavior.
13. Poor memory and concentration.
14. Change in personality.
15. Feeling "followed."
16. Feeling "drained."
17. Erratic physical aches and pains.
18. Nightmares with the inability to distinguish fantasy from reality.
19. Schizophrenia.
20. Guilt and remorse.
21. General paranoia/anxiety.
22. Hearing inner voices with negative messages.

SYMPTOMS OF SPIRIT POSSESSION

1. Negative emotional or physical reactions to the idea of spiritual detox (*part* of you wanting it, the other *part* of you not wanting it).
2. Physical, emotional, mental, and spiritual senses feeling "blocked."
3. You drank. You did drugs.
4. Sudden compulsive desires.
5. Inexplicable perspiration.
6. Sensing an unexplainable presence in your home, especially while falling asleep or when waking up in the middle of the night.
7. Insomnia.
8. Sudden and mysterious strife and conflict with loved ones.
9. Nausea and vomiting.
10. Addiction to sex.
11. Sudden onset of sadness, depression.
12. Reckless behavior.
13. Poor memory and concentration.
14. Change in personality.
15. Feeling "followed."
16. Feeling "drained."
17. Erratic physical aches and pains.
18. Nightmares with the inability to distinguish fantasy from reality.
19. Schizophrenia.
20. Guilt and remorse.
21. General paranoia/anxiety.
22. Hearing inner voices with negative messages.

PART
ONE

ONE

While these three grey brick walls and steel bars before me will serve as harsh reminders that I should know better, they also reassure me that I have all the time in the world. So, I will attempt to distill any evaporated fumes of my innocence in order to retell the following. Allow me to regress into my former younger, more naive self for a moment, the same way one might channel the voice of a young boy, singing a song to calm his nerves before realizing the song may naturally refrain into the most desperate, unattainable wish the world has ever denied.

It was a rye summer that would soon blossom into a juniper berry fall. From one season to the next, the sun would always set on the backside of good fortune, but never rise to reveal any, as we insisted on living in a microcosm of silhouette. My roommates Luis, Bobby and I received a Three Day Or Quit on our apartment door after an incident involving one of our gang's more thuggish bullies and the pregnant lady next door. It was in one of those future ghetto gated-communities so we considered our expulsion to be in everyone's best interest.

But the clock's imposing presence was the only sure thing. It was only a matter of time. We were doomed to settle for the first place we could find. On the pacing, hair-pulling eve of the second night of residential purgatory, not even music or drink could help soothe the mood. Luis' girlfriend spotted a steal of a pad – a two bedroom with a garage, just a block from the beach and on top of a liquor store for just under $900. Not squandering a second, we raced down there within the hour.

After procuring the keys from the liquor store owner, a fast-talking Vietnamese man, we were briefly hoodwinked into a distracting sales pitch as he tried selling us one of his baby alligators in shattered English. Walking backwards in polite decline we then climbed a shoddy, salt-eroded flight of stairs. We had already decided it was our new apartment before we had laid eyes on it. Luis and I approached the door and slowly creaked it open. The moment was pure living cinema when the two of us looked at one another after scanning the perimeter, slack-jawed by the instantly stifling, oppressive vibrations of the place. Nothing visual could bring on a feeling like this... as if we had walked into an invisible but living, breathing static channel where you are scared – too scared to move – and you don't, can't, and won't know why.

We did our best to laugh it off. I forced a smile when I called Luis and Bobby over to the kitchen. I had discovered the fridge, well stocked with at least three days worth of wine and beer. We immediately began draining the assumed amenities as we continued to peruse, making flippantly sick Vietnam war jokes that the *Charlie* downstairs had led us into some death-trap. With six wandering eyes on the ceiling, one could assume we were already looking for a way out, though we knew we had passed the point of no return. We went back downstairs, handed him the cash and the apartment was ours, no questions asked besides the growing list we had for ourselves.

With only two bedrooms to the three of us, I elected myself to take the dining room as my sheet-curtained quarters, nearly missing the perfect circle of dead flies smack dab in the center of the room. Even through its calculated geometry I thought nothing beyond its trivial neglected filth. Luis broke the inconsequence as he entered the room, pointing down to this curious display while gasping a descending "Oh nooo…" as if he had just heard the worst news of his life.

"You know what that is, don't you?"

Intercepting any chance of reply he immediately dove into an absurd but admittedly unnerving history of the *Halo Of Flies*, the theory of maggots and flies as indication of satanic presence. Regardless of this sensationalistic rant that was getting more claustrophobically dorky by the second, the fact remained: We were terrified, by our very breath, our anxious eyes, all touched by something untouchable that had managed to find its way into the increasingly rare moments where nothing unusual was happening.

Reluctantly, we moved in the next day. I would have never closed my eyes had I known what kind of torturous slumber was in store for the three of us that following evening. These weren't just nightmares resulting from a collective archetypical fear we had that night, as much as it was an endless, beginning-less myriad of paralyzing torment masquerading as dreamscape. After falling into a mile-deep sleep, I suddenly found myself submerged in the vibrations of some otherworldly voice. A silencing envelopment akin to finding oneself alone in the middle of the Atlantic trying to stay afloat, both the depth and width inconceivable. A voice that spoke slowly, repeating with intensity the words…

MOVE OUT

…until it became a ceaseless mantra dissolving into nerve-shattering nonsense. This continued steadily for hours until I finally found the strength to pry my eyes open and then… silence.

A view of my room, now curiously empty. All of my belongings and half-unpacked boxes gone, as if they had never arrived. I quickly understood that what I was seeing was what my room, the whole apartment, looked like before our residency. I couldn't move

my head to investigate further. I was experiencing that strange paralysis when one is halfway between waking and dreaming. Between
the physical and the invisible. Where one is completely aware of his
surroundings but unable to move, talk or scream. I realized I had
inadvertently detoured into some alternate dimension of our apartment sometime before we moved in. Victim to magnetism pulling
my feeble attention to the darkened corner of our living room where
there lay such a dominant presence I could not focus on in the inanimate state I had found myself in.

Eventually I awoke, wholly convinced I had been awake all
night. I called my father immediately. I knew he would give advice
beyond the normal skeptic parental rhetoric, as I always considered
him a mystic of sorts - a veteran of LSD, practitioner of transcend-
ental meditation and scholar of the esoteric lexicon. He would be
the last one to scoff at such a dilemma. We spoke over one another
as he attempted calming interjections. Perhaps he didn't realize the
severity of the situation after dealing with his bat-shit son who
suffered from chronic panic attacks, most likely due to the
comedown of being raised in that Heaven on Earth cult. I pleaded
that there was no possible delusion in this instance. He suggested inviting all our closest friends to the new place with the objective to
inundate the apartment with familiarity, positive re-enforcement,
etc. I couldn't help but roll my eyes at the suggestion, the idea of
positivity being a nearly impossible concept for anyone I associate
with. Still, his order was to rid the place of the stale, dead air and to
conjure up whatever vibrancy we could. I had no choice but to follow, saluting, smirking.

He concluded, "Try this, if you don't notice a difference and still
have problems the next day call me and I'll have further instruc-
tions..."

We had an impromptu housewarming that night, not really di-
vulging what went down the previous evening, yet putting urgent

emphasis that everyone's attendance was mandatory. All the co-ed young adult harlots came in fierce battalion, armed with libations as they attempted to settle in. I quickly noticed that not one person could sit down and relax. They just paced back and forth, looking down, looking up, bursts of nervous laughter with forced one-liners and perplexed expressions forming on their faces.

Attention soon turned outside to a splintered group talking to our friend Nick, a thirteen year-old premature delinquent and younger brother of Max, one of our contemporaries. Nick recently returned home after having ran away for two months. While usually eager to hang with us *elders*, there seemed to be a reason wasn't coming inside to join the increasingly awkward party. Instead, he was holding court to the ones in earshot in a tense conversation, everyone surrounded him trying to pry something out as he spoke, half with his hands, mouth agape, eyes occasionally peering up at the apartment. I thought nothing of it until Max came up stairs.

"You really need to come downstairs, man. I think you should lend an ear to my brother. Right now."

It was common knowledge among our circle that Nick had been missing for a solid three weeks during the two months he had run away. When he finally surfaced, he only vaguely eluded to a beachside apartment where he had stayed, though any specific whereabouts were never spilled until this moment. He seemed to have an agenda to keep this location shrouded, although no one could tell whether his motives were a sworn pact to protect his harboring coven or to hide post-traumatic residue. Either way, the subject had been left alone, the kid not budging until this instant, where he proceeded to tell us that it was *this* apartment where he had stayed. The previous tenants he described as "weird satanists."

It was an easy accusation for our sect of absolute heathens to scoff at. Doing a bit of tall-tale damage control I asked Nick to describe in explicit detail the layout of our apartment from the entry where he stood. He passed the test with flying colors, ending his wild gestured architectural review with the dining room. My room. Here he claimed they performed the rituals, where they would go into trance-type chanting, conjuring spirits and giving them offerings in the form of certain obscene endeavors. These he refused to describe. Regardless, one could tell that whatever his role in this clandestine coven truly was, it was something that had punctured him deeply. It was better we not pick at that scar. We did our best to kill our curiosity out of respect for the kid, but this could not stifle our growing sense of slow-burning panic.

Everyone upstairs screamed.

The girls ran out to the porch in shivering unease, eyes to the ground in shame-tainted disbelief. The guys still inside bellowing various exclamations, drowned out by our stomping footsteps on the stairs. The lights had suddenly gone out, back on, followed by random inanimate violence in the kitchen and maybe the bathroom – cupboards banging, glasses shattering – all the storybook haunted house clichés becoming real.

We ran upstairs to assess the frenzy. The brave, or drunkenly numb, began to relay what had just happened. Those outside had the forced opportunity to join in the choir of screaming, each of our wails providing nothing beyond kindling to the chaos. The whole crowd evacuated with barely a goodbye. The *party* was over. Our own howling rendered any potential police sirens superfluous.

Now left to the unlucky three of us again, the proud new tenants. Too rattled and obsessed to sleep in the apartment, we got on the phone to track down alternate pads to crash at for the remainder of this fractured evening. I ran to my folks' house less than a mile away to consult my father. Once again, my makeshift mystic. When I arrived he read the severity in my stuttering. He re-directed me to do it all over again, but this time we would be armed with a specific task.

He explained, "First thing in the morning you go right down to the store, get rubbing alcohol, a carton of Epsom salt. I will give you some camphor - I have left over from my initiations. Now, in every room of your apartment you're to place a small plate or saucer in the middle of the floor. Pour about two tablespoons of the Epsom salt onto the plate, then top it off with the rubbing alcohol, so the salt is just submerged enough to turn into a kind of soupy paste. Have everyone in the house focus their energy into this solution as you drop a match and it ignites. Watch the flame. As the flame dies down it essentially sucks all the corrupt presence along with it. Burn the camphor as well. It will fill the room with its cleansing odor. I imagine your apartment smells pretty bad. Repeat this in each room. You're going to notice one room's flame to be higher than the others. When you see that flame, when it stands out from the others, this is the room you must focus on most."

The next morning I called Luis and Bobby along with everyone in our inner circle. I persuaded them to do it all over again, this time with my father's do-it-yourself spirit cleansing stunt backing us. I assigned certain people with the strongest personalities to each room, initiating a youthful vibrancy to activate some kind of deliberate shift, with me spearheading the campaign.

It started out as the feel good event of the summer. The three of us had cracked the Gordon's Gin to balance our bracing anticipation. We paced back and forth, riffing how the Gordon's emblem resembled a demon, but there was only so much mileage we could get out of that one. A parade of daring smiles came through the door in single file, our friends already stumbling from an obvious head start. The crowd's chatter grew to a fevered pitch. Everyone's way of dealing with the nail-biting atmosphere was to make defiant sarcastic wisecracks, prompting me to announce the commencing of our simulated homespun exorcism, where I, the victimized host, would enter each room with said ingredients, lighting the fuckers on fire. I

welcomed whoever wanted to join me, resulting in a huddled, fo-
cused procession while the rest of the party continued.

I was on my fifth gin and tonic when we got started. We began
in the living room, the starting / finishing line. I prepared the soupy
solution in the middle of our camouflage-stained carpet in front of
an enthralled audience of slurring harlots. I threw a match in the
saucer.

The flame shot up about a foot, about right for the amount of alcohol I had designated to add each time. This trend did not deviate
drastically from room to room until I got to my own.

I repeated the procedure. To our horror, the flame shot up quick,
violent, and pushed the four-foot mark.

*"When you see that flame, when it stands out from the others, this is the
room you must focus on most."*

I woke up the next morning with an upside-down rat's eye view
of Luis's face looking down on me. He shook his head in sympathetic shame.

"They got you, man."

"What? What's that supposed to mean?" I creaked out.

"They just got you man. They got you," he said as he slowly
walked away.

TWO

My stomach swelled with each of Luis' somber steps. Unprecedented dread. I turned over and realized I was on my porch, deserted besides all the bottles, the other fallen soldiers. I peeled myself up and went inside. He just stared at me, shaking his head as he sat me down to begin to spill it.

Apparently, after the flame in my room had finally died down, I began the whole process again, starting from the living room. But as I continued in each room, my behavior grew increasingly obsessive and erratic. I eventually ditched the whole ritual and began to run clockwise a good six to seven revolutions throughout the apartment on the same path I had been treading for the last hour or so, until I finally returned to the living room where I frantically tried to scale the walls, scratching at the paint like a freshly trapped insect. Soon thereafter I started climbing the furniture, trying to get to the highest vistas. I hoisted myself on the arm of the couch and perched, surveying the room. I was speaking a language that clearly was not English, alternating my attention between friends. I zeroed in on a new face with every brief pause in the babble. Some laughed, others oozed nervous concern. I jumped off, only to scramble to the top of a teetering bookshelf, continuing the same archaic spouting before going for the top of the TV set where my volume grew the loudest. Attendees were well beyond hysterical at this point. Someone tried to play hero and did their best to get me down, but to no success, as I screamed further nonsensical scathing, swinging my arms in front of me. Any motive of whether it was in defense or offense was blurred in its sheer rapidity. Luis said it was around this time that three or more people snuck out the door without a goodbye. Concurrent, I jumped off the TV and ran clockwise around the house again, gurgling obscenities, busting through the crowd with their every attempt to close in. This madness continued for another four or five circles until I got to the living room, but instead of stopping there I zig-zagged out the door to the porch, losing the crowd. I zeroed in on our friend Keith who had just arrived at the top of the stairs. As if he was were as light as a loaf of bread, I picked him up over my head and threw him down our flight of stairs, a jagged twelve foot drop to the bottom. He landed on his back with a fleshy thud, groaning in agony as he tried to pick himself up. He stood erect and immediately fell over again, holding his shaking head with both hands flat on his temples before limping away toward the main road as others scattered after him. They had all realized they were nowhere safe. All those that stayed behind just kept groaning, pointing, covering their mouths as they watched the others pounce and tackle me down the stairs. It took roughly six fists to knock me out cold, putting an end to my continuous thrashing. "This is a goddamned rodeo!" someone laughed, cruelly. I was carried back up to the porch and laid down. They were apprehensive to touch me anymore than they had to. They locked the front door as I lay there, finally inanimate.

Luis sighed once more after explaining the night to me, its legitimate victim, still shaking his head as he walked back inside, mumbling some sort of backhanded apology. My stomach dropped like a hammer as I allowed it to sink in. I tried to counteract the sensation by attempting to cease to exist. Surging anxiety imploded into unnerving twitches. I could not blame or regret any punishment I had or would receive. I was inviting it with open arms, despite contrary grimacing, so jugular-bulging it was simultaneously warding off justice.

A split second of calm made me ponder the day of the week. Sunday, I decided. Church!!! Isn't that what they do, the last resort of the irreparably damned?!? Isn't that what I should do?

CHURCH!!! It's probably somewhere out there right now! Surrounded by darkness there is a light, with a force to push you through that light like a cube being grated through a triangular hole. A force that cracks and compromises, created solely from your helplessness, pushing you into the solemn chamber with all the broken, disfigured vessels that came before you. This was surrender. Emergency. I was prepared to take back every curse I had ever screamed to God, every satisfying, perfectly angled fuck I had on every cold tombstone as a teen, every heathen howl at the moon while we ran through fire, every drop of poison I had ever hurled down my throat... Clearly, I am a monster, born and bred, but I was going to allow that light to impale me in all its burning glory. Should I die of shock, then I have well overstayed my welcome.

I had to find a suit immediately! At every funeral and wedding I had been to, the men wore suits, and I wanted to be a man. Beyond those kind of formal occasions and some random heartfelt acts of vandalism, I had never been to church. I had also never worn a suit. Luckily, my brief fling with a chipped-toothed beauty named Jackie yielded some souvenirs other than shivers and confusion. Her Mother had taken such a liking to me that she thought I deserved no less than eleven gaudy suits left behind by their recently deceased neighbor. Quickly retrieved from a squashed trash bag on the floor where it should have remained, I tried on the least descript but no less hideously oversized double-breasted nightmare. Not wasting a second, I proceeded down the street on foot, walking three miles to the only church I could think of. The same church where a close friend trumped all of our previous stunts by hucking a Molotov Cocktail on the roof as he throttled by on his motorcycle. His napalmed victory quickly became the stuff of hushed legend.

I folded and rolled up the cuffs as I walked, makeshift tailoring it to my own emaciated specifications, quickly achieving the look of a shipwrecked Wall Street wing nut. I walked past the white-on-black plastic lettered marquee, which looked more like integrity's tomb-stone. I descended down a staircase. I took a stuttered breath while gingerly thumbing the latch of the wood and wrought-iron double-door, knowing I would likely be joining the ceremony in progress.

There was of course no relief here, only further stoking of still-smoldering brimstone. With every mephitic step I took down that aisle I felt another unforgiving eye fixate on me, followed by various whispers quickly graduating to white noise. Looks of horror and gasping confusion, some slack-jawed pseudo-sympathy and shaking heads. Some even tried to smile, only forgetting to conceal their fangs. I found a seat I thought was a safe distance from the nerve-shattering nucleus. They all looked like corpses! If they weren't senior citizens knocking on death's door, they looked like they had given up regardless, pale and drained, mourning in perfect time with the pastor's alarm-clock climaxes. He spoke not of love, salvation and forgiveness but of death, impending destruction, and macabre consequence. He quickly sent my simmering panic into crippling consternation, filling my exempt guts with such venomous steam that I exploded into the most piercing squall, resonating the whole chamber, strangling every splinter of wood, every shard of stained-glass, every molecule of low-hanging misty residue of the preacher's putrid words.

"FFUUUUUUUUUUUUUUUUUUUUUUUUUUUUUUU UUUUUAAACK!!!"

The throes of some unholy epilepsy thrust my feet into the crowded pew, rocking, then finally lifting it off the ground, dumping them all like dirt.

I saw the light. I kicked and screamed.

PART
TWO

ONE

I tapped you on the shoulder from behind. I could see you didn't immediately perceive the touch to be from an actual finger, the way you tried to brush it off with the aloof care of someone dealing with an insect.

But you were alone.

We are always alone.

Even back in all those cafeterias and dancehalls you wondered why you were the only one sitting alone at such a large empty table, with not a curious or even pitiful eye to be offered your way, being kept in cold company by the abandoned cups and all their congealing dew drops of fruit punch. Though it was always people like us, us alone who actually made the conscious decision to sit away from the numbers.

I sense that there might be a vapor of reluctance where soon there will be trust. Maybe this was not such a good idea. But we have come this far and I am not one for pleasantries that would only make us more anxious. So, perhaps as a sort of detour of consolation we can forget the present, if for just a moment. Act as though this isn't even happening while submitting yourself entirely.

Let me ask... Do you ever really stop to ponder the solid discrepancies, if any, between memory and imagination? In moments of retrospection, imagination is an essential ingredient to communicate, and ultimately immortalize, any profundity that might be otherwise lost. This must apply, whether we are recounting an experience to others, or simply reminding ourselves of such a moment. With this - an atmosphere - an ethereal undercurrent or actual life-force is unconsciously obtained, possibly activated by something as trivial as a facial expression, a certain word, the mood of a word spoken, a specific twist in the scenery. All this can claim dominion over the recollection and ultimately the recipient of the memory. It then quickly turns contagion to the listener as it is retold, and if recited correctly, can successfully possess the listener, almost identical to the effect it had on the first person. Time comes to a standstill. Most voluntary brain-activity becomes paralytic, left only with a dementia-riddled submission to the anatomy of this freeze frame, where one could be brought to tears, locked staring into distant, unsettlingly familiar eyes.

This said, it frightens me how easily I could just throw myself crashing through the nearest window when I think of their perception of dreams. The ho-hum ungrateful, indeed unimaginative masses who will dismiss our nocturnal journeys as a mere dumping of unneeded information we have gathered throughout the day. The quaint ignorance to try to interpret these dreams? Well, I would equate that to finding a hidden meaning in something as deliberate as a cold-blooded stabbing, random or otherwise; where the idea, intent, action and results are so naked in their exhibition, so soaked in their own blood that one could become a laughing shadow in their cul-de-sac analysis!

So, it is you that I condemn to extra-special dreams tonight! Where you will bear witness to a lover you have never met before dying slowly, before your crying pleading eyes in which you promptly "wake up" sobbing in the exact same hysterics! Where you are being tickled by various violating hands, making you shriek in a certain panic vomiting laughter that carries you to the waking world still giggling uncontrollably! In which an inexplicable force seduces you to the edge of a tall building, as you immediately swan-dive without thinking of the rushing consequence! The wind of your plummet assaulting every inch of you, your heart jack-hammering against your chest, out-racing your free fall, beating so voraciously you can feel it rattling your ribcage as you wake up, a safe landing on your bed!!!

Having been reminded that you still have a pulse, I challenge you to still chortle foolishly on any remaining differences, dwarfed in the presence of what has been there all along.

We leave behind gold-dust trails, like comets, forever altering the environment, making even the inanimate stand at Gestapo-observant attention, igniting atmospheres we could cut with a knife. Should we have the guts to dissect it? Should another person pass through where we have just left our mark, may they be susceptible enough to our residue, raw-nerved enough to wonder, suspended, unapologetic. May each catastrophic step they take through our brittle pinball histories have a mousetrap tension; the tighter our springs, the faster they snap out of our crude, narrow crawlspace.

Yet this heavy stepping isn't altogether clumsy, nor can I blame my legs for the erratic paths they tread. As my speech and path become independently out of synch, there seems to be some kind of puppeteer behind my gesticulating. A force propelling my ignorant blood outward. Blood that believes outside the artery walls lies nothing but outer space, true escape. It must only find its way out of this maze. When the soul is on fire and screaming to be extinguished, it is with the dousing of alcohol where it is not exactly diminished, but instead made to conjure a combustive smolder. Smoke rising, not out of a death, but in a determined distribution, following the vapor. It pours into me, through me, my trail of scorched earth impossible to argue with, as all witnesses trip over their charred lower lips.

TWO

What is it about winter that makes our scarred-over hearts squeal for liquor? We shiver like orphans, abandoned to the elements. Clumsily we test our last ounce of strength as we swing down the sledge on that bell at the carnival, catapulting our imagination into that ascending aluminum ball we naively mistake for our own temperature rising. We go a long way with this well-intentioned delusion. One grand epiphany induced by this edible ether – whatever forms it takes, we'll take. We lift something heavy again, this time to our lips. In tenacious waves it floods first our mouth, playfully flashing though every pore while diminishing all dormant complaints stillborn in the gate of our throat. We unconsciously hold it there like a dam, refusing to let the initial warming of our skull end - but only for the most undocumented hair-split second before we allow this lava do its real work – its medicinal descent down the sieve of our windpipe, avalanching, coating, rushing to every deprived trembling cell, each taking the role of an egg and the spirits the sperm, longing to complete each other in the eternal tail-eating drama. A metamorphosis has taken place. We are warm, our fists are clenched, and we are ready to swing again!

What is it about spring? Now that we are finally warming up, ice turning into glistening pools, birdsong no longer choked by the chill, blooming botanical births from each suspended seed. We still howl for alcohol. This time it is means for celebration, not emergency. We are now wholly conscious - we have realized it was the coldest winter to date and we have survived. What else would be more appropriate than to indulge in what made this all possible? Now we drink with a full heart and virginal eyes, taking in the Technicolor scenery. The world looks even brighter with every sip of this fresh nectar!

But a fresh eye is not exempt from spoiling! Emotional moisture that may threaten tears of joy gives life to any pregnant spore on our cornea. Our sips quickly grow to gulps, our goblets to gallons, our gift to greed, wanting to hold the world suspended in such perfect utopian display that we clumsily shatter the glass case it's presented in. We remove it, hugging it until we tremble. Here is when summer comes. This time the answer is in the question. We don't stop to think or even casually relish, as we have been overcome – abducted even - by the very spirit in which we sought to seek commiseration. The warmth we once craved has cracked into an unbearable heat, browning the grasses, drying the lakes, burning our skin. Again, our only escape is to continue this flooding of the soul inside the human buoy. Gaunt, we now resemble a skeleton, as the alcohol seems to flow right out our ribcage, or trickle through our pelvis and some-times right back into the cup again.

Our thirst never quenched. Parties go on for days and this, in and of itself, is the nucleus of the special occasion. No one cares that you were born or how old you are, as long as you are alive enough to lift the sweating brim to your chapped lips. The Sun has become the enemy, threatening to boil our beloved brew until its penultim-ate evaporation. We retaliate by drinking as fast as we can until the...

Fall. We now have a worm's eye view of the compromised trees that could have sheltered us in summer. Their leaves teasingly fall in slow motion, implying our own hovering recognizance. Whatever was up is now down, begging to join us in our descent. The only way to soften this premature night is with more alcohol, to abstruse all borders of contrast and make what has spiraled out of control even more sub-real. We are spun with the wind into blurred leper dervishes, settling again where we couldn't care less. With every sip we egg on the death of the day, knowing comfort in the anonymity of a depth obscured. Slurring in sterling tongue riddles, realizations ignorant and not meant for anyone but our own droning choir. Fall ushers in the endings of the festival to make room for more private explorations of Saturnalian endurance.

I remember the ground rushing up to meet my silent face, limbs flying wildly as if grabbing thin air would somehow break my fall. I had made usual rounds, retreating to the most pitch-black corners of the neighborhood, so attracted to something they held, a brain-eating hunch that something was always waiting for me in the most labyrinthine paths of dead air, the sheer blindness of it all becoming aphrodisiac. This pheromone magnetism led me to a junkyard of sorts in a deep crater of the surface streets, behind shadows of shadows, through bottomless cornea-tricking black static delight. It was a storage lot for movie props – bathtubs, toilets, cars, dressers, wet bars, grand-dad clocks, all stacked and teetering in imperfect rows or half-fallen, creating a wondrous circuit of tunnels for someone as drunk and adrenaline-sick as I. My drinking began at noon and was now entering a zone where time did not exist. I had my red headed girlfriend with me and had already hit her in the face, and the mere thought of why she was still by my side was making me even dizzier. By the time she tried to convince me, in vain, that there was nothing in the recesses of this angular ocean of inconsequential artifact, I was already swallowed up. Her voice became a mere echo as I panted feverishly, a gold miner on all fours insisting on the most dead-end direction away from any and all shine. I could no longer justify myself a moth seduced by the light, preferring all-knowing rodent, molesting all mystery.

An evasive flash of streetlight triggered my ascent back to the streets of human garbage. I knew no obligation to find any kind of vague camaraderie with them, as never before could a festival conjure up this much hate and violation inside me. Through their eyes they would be simply strolling, but in mine they were trolling. Their collective laughter took on a discordant conspiring cackle, and with every deceivingly harmless movement, they would form a barricade in my path. I had to exit this noxious scene, the last sane cell in me policing my balled fists into my pockets and my bowed legs on the imaginary line home. That chain-link wall, towering yet feeble, with all those diamond holes of possibility, was the only thing separating me from freedom and further pin-balling by the rapids of this bohemophiliac stream. It could have been pure brick and mortar and I would have still found a way to walk through as a ghost, which I was on my way to becoming. Dark skinned musclemen in yellow jackets had other ideas for me, further jumbling my agitated frequencies, telling me the exit was the entrance. And should I try to pass through they would take me down. So, it was clear. No choice but up.

Who would create this crucifying display of a generation drowned in some gawking aquarium? I am a man, not a fish! I have arms, legs, and a sizzling fuse surrounded by fire! I ran toward the fence for my final ascent when hands came all over me, a public molestation for all to witness in their hypnotized pussyfoot paralysis. They all gasped like we were fireworks as the violence turned consensual. My torso swiveled as my fist swung behind me, while the free hand threw the rest of myself onto the fence to see what would stick. Everything adhered as I shoved one boot in any sympathetic hole while kicking them off me with the other. I reached for the top, pulling the rest of my body up. Now a smirking gargoyle about to show the audience what it meant to fly.

My destination was not for the stars but for the cold unforgiving ground. Not only did I jump... I twisted, turning airborne like an epileptic high diver, hearing jagged screams from the crowd below, moaning from all directions as the ground rushed up. I managed one last spastic revolution, finally landing limp on my back and the side of my imploding face. I heard rubber on asphalt stampeding as adrenaline reanimated my near-corpse. I rose like a tin man and ran

up the hill for my life like a suffocating, slow motion nightmare running in hungry sand, making every last cracked cell work one more
time against their will. Right now everything was the enemy. I deflated right where the horizon bites the sky, reduced to a silhouette
of wheezing gray matter.

Leveled to this sort of subtraction, my whole being was still determined to compete with the skyline itself. Paralleled by, but non-
etheless planked on the lowest rung. I lay there part of the pavement
and even this was not enough, no more comfort in clenched fists as
they quickly became claws and, physics be damned, began to
scrape, dig, and fiend at the immortal cement, ripping fingernails
then ultimately flesh - concluding my losing battle, where the
ground had instead dug into me. I laid there surrendering, sobbing,
ignorant to motives, confused whether I was trying to excavate a
hole to bury myself or was I territorially pissing my final mark on
the night, finger painting my last masterpiece in sacrificial gore?
Who needs a reason when the intention, and for that matter the opposition, was this solid.

I awake in fetal position, hands in my leg pits, the itchy prick of
the grass a bed of nails. Raising one eyelid, its concealed ball slowly
followed up to a sky that was spinning out of control, akin to the
view of what the ground might look like to a skydiver miles up -
only that man would have the luxury of a parachute to whip such
hazard into a safer, slower, more streamlined descent. I, on the other
hand, am going the other direction altogether, starting from the unforgiving Earth and now falling into the bottomless, lidless sky in
voracious vertigo. The ground where I laid is pushing me... I could
close my eyes but then the vast static would quickly form tangible
images of demonic heads exploding, dark recess sex torture of the
most inconceivable depredates, and God forbid - my own face. No.
Most thoughts are involuntary but these have no organic origin; the
only sense I can make is that they are being thrust upon me by an

unknown entity. Stratosphere still spinning, I try looking lazily towards the opposite direction of the taunting revolution, counterclockwise then quickly back clockwise, as it slows to a series of skipping, blurring 3D afterimages. The guts churn until the bile boils. There is no escape, even when you are falling into something as wide open as the sky itself. This is not a hallucination. At best, it will pass, but only after its full puppet-string manipulation of time, making one frightfully analyze each second until it cruelly stretches out into minutes, becoming longer, stronger, spiral staircase deeper with each tremor. I ask myself, "Am I cold or just convulsing?" not wanting to know the answer. Foraging for any vague happenstance of temporary suicide - should I actually be given a bird's eye view of my empty vessel like they show in the movies and explain in metaphysics, I know I would quickly wish it permanent, as I ask myself in volcanic agony, though I have known it a million times - how did this happen?

THREE

I am thirty-one years old. For a second I am amazed how this all seems like yesterday until I realized it actually was. But it could have been any time in the past fifteen years. You could say I am wiser now but only because at this very moment I know myself too well. But acquiring wisdom should never be equated with being cured, and having a specific insight will often be more of a burden than a life of ignorance. Where some could maybe boast with this breed of epiphany, I can only mourn the same way I do every time I am invited out on the town, already knowing how it will all end. Feeling the sheer weight of this truth begin to crack my bones, the pressure creating magnetism towards the ground. The more I resist, the more I hear the splitting of marrow, the tearing of tendons, until the pain becomes so great that I wonder what it is exactly that I have to gain by struggling against the inevitable.

I preemptively strike with alcohol! Not to destroy or even deny this hindrance, but to dilute, to make it settle softly, at times even allowing it to penetrate more deeply, but only after I have admitted the first round of defeat.

My actual *condition* is often confused with my natural gravitation towards intoxication. The reality is far more complex, something you will not find the answer to in any kind of manual, textbook, twelve-step program or any of their coffee-stained Bibles. When you are truly sick do you blame the medicine? It is something airborne no doubt, something you cannot touch.

It is clear to me that I am a man possessed by an ill-willed spirit that has played me like a crooked brown-note trumpet for as long as I can recall. I will call this *The Intrusion.*

If it is proof that you want, then it's proof that you'll get every time I steer myself to a moment of inspired divine contentment. It is not my *will* that captains the sudden exodus out of this perfect place. The bottle is lifted, emptied, then right before my gracious yet horrified eyes it is magically replenished by an unseen hand, like an hourglass which turns *me* upside-down.

I strike the bull's eye. That isolated, frozen moment where one steps outside their slave-driving ego to bear witness to this beautiful crawling anthill of a universe - only to realize, even just for one escapist's second, that everything has its place, that you are right where you need to be. A part of some grand cause and effect, like the actual bubbles in your drink in their bee-lining thrust to the surface where they jump, pop and fall into a collective playful mist. Yes, for one moment in our suffocating routines we are actually allowed to breathe with this, to briefly remind ourselves what it was like.

But every breath past this glorious point is where *The Intrusion* takes place, gagging every inhalation. Flash flood. Who, I ask, in his right mind would not choose to simply walk away from that previous moment of cosmic validation, refreshed and relieved!?! I submit my form to being a vital spoke of the roulette and somehow allow this Spirit inside, the same Spirit that performs this malicious witch-doctor miracle of turning the cure into a poison far more ravaging than the meager threat of disillusionment I began with. What was first a world brighter than I ever imagined quickly takes on a suspicious wash. Best friend's faces morphing with the darkness into secret expressions of doubt, using my embodiment as a reflective pool where one does not see the sky but instead the blindness that will follow.

The Blackout happens to be the luckiest part of this saga. I am left with no memory of the thrashings I have dished out and been served. I could, with instinctual ease, convince myself that nothing happened, that the night went on like the fairytales it was meant to pantomime – only I will awake to shadows of lynch mobs who arrive to teach me otherwise. This ill Spirit turns my comrades into enemies, but only unsafe in the confines of my own wet-brain. The reality outside of my skull is far more disturbing – they have all actually stopped caring one way or the other. My bones creak, commencing collapse, unless I find one last surge of adrenaline to run and hide like a cat about to die. I extinguish my phone, turn off the lights, cut out my own tongue, take ice cream scoopers to my eyes. The Spirit's voices soon enter, symphonic layers moaning the mantra of doom-laden inevitable. These messages always come with hallucinatory visual-aids on a loop – hearts impaled, heads exploding, oceans of demonic faces occupying my periphery, any attempt to shut my eyes only revealing them lurking in the shadow, boasting their impending potential.

Do you see this cannot be me? Not even the most depraved soldiers of sadomasochistic war crimes would consciously summon this breed of abuse. No one in his right mind, I said! The paradox always goes one step further with the rationalization that I am indeed not in my right mind.

This thick skin is imaginary, more like an exposed mass of raw nerve susceptible to anything, willing, screaming for it even. Sensitive to the most minor tremors, reactive to the slightest shift of wind, my responding shivers mimicking the movement, awakening ruminations of the deepest internal reaches. The Santa Anas form from a clash of warmth, cold, and third eye anticipation, bringing these familiar overwhelming waves of curiosity, discontent and undeniable ruin. Voices are muffled until our wide eyes do the talking. This wind seems to create a vast web of electricity, connecting all pulsing chaos of this uncommon city of Los Angeles into a surging circuit board, as if painted by Bosch. A sprawling tornado with you as the eye, the center of this metropolitan drain-whirl as all directions slowly close in. A grave deception is tempered here – we are convinced everything we want is close within reach, and should we miss the grab, we'll surely get it on the next revolution. We ignore the gravitational pull. We mistake the horizon rising for the curtains coming up for our show time. But we are sinking. We cannot walk through solid ground, and our audience has since fled for their own safety. Even the most stubborn of palm trees begin to bend towards the horizon in a display of all natural torture. Our stomachs have learned to drop at the thought even, though not out of cowardice. It takes guts to be this far prone.

Within in a day or two of self-imposed prohibition, when I am in my more lucid moments - born not out of any instinct of health or maintenance but a quaking fear - I still end up a man possessed. Whether it's conversations with strangers, friends, or myself, I am effortlessly elevated by vague twinges of excitement or despair, quickly animating me. I can only surrender to this ruffling of feathers, encouraging its contagion. Should it not be met with a mutual glow, then I am quicker than a cockroach, not walking as much as I am vacillating, as if the more ground and open air I cover the faster I might crash into potential participants. There is no passing scenery with me - all is pliable and waiting to capture me and I it, hyper aware like the two sides of a gun duel itching to make a move just to get the morbid outcome finished.

The skin is a two-way mirror, my soul the authoritative voyeur in this indictment of environment where there is only mimicry to enforce the whittling down of this vast victim, no questions, no interrogation. Everything reveals itself and everything speaks, even the inanimate. I see myself in the deadest, most brittle-brown leaf that falls from the tree, miming its movements, fluttering in its last plunge that defying any tic-tock, dancing to invisible rhythms playfully flipping this way and that, submissive to the wind, making the most out of that deceiving, mocking plummet.

While this all may sound like something borderline whimsical, open hearted and perhaps even utopian... Well, this is just the start of a jagged path that is typically laid, arriving at its dizzying and ultimately blinding finale.

FOUR

It has been said many times, and with no stubborn opposition from me, that I keep an unsavory company. I have always met these condemnations with what can only be explained as a hybrid of concurrence and pride, a distinct solidarity with the persecuted pack in question. I cannot deny: their piercing of atmospheres, the deep footprints they leave, their dangling rags, their ear-shattering heresies, their salivating smiles, the silencing, their abysmal shadows, or their annihilating lust for drink and revelry - anymore than I can deny my warped reflection when I look them dead in the eyes. One merely has to look upon any congregation of this crowd to save the analytical stalemate of trying in vain to strip me of my layers. You could die wondering, finally out of breath from every curse you conjure, of why and how we exist, where our morals have gone, and what exactly has contaminated our life-blood. But through every opposition we still will inevitably gravitate toward each other like bubbles in a piss-pot!

In spite of our magnetic tendencies the erupting individual in each of us is impenetrable. As we converge, we are ever more alone in our prison of personalities, yet it advances, elevating our egos to far more dizzying heights where only the continual thinning of our boiling blood can bring us back down.

We were young and only saw the world as a gaping, dripping-jawed mouth where we could dive into the process, bypassing all hypothesis. We met, as most misfits do, getting crushed into the corners where walls meet, as the rest of the world continues its trivial spin. This created an attractive vertical obscurity. One that never quite dead-ended, akin to the divine vagina from which we were all torn. One by one we appeared in these places in adolescent stumble, aloof, no trite pleasantries or obligatory welcome – one merely had to make eye contact to understand we were from the same tribe, nod knowingly, as we walked deeper into the shade of darker trespass.

But not to ignore initiation! Fate is only to be trusted as far as you or the others can puncture their own skin! Should we be content to be just another crowd when there are clearly further caverns to spelunk?!? The first time I saw you I already knew not all of us would make it. Regardless of the future, it was time to get curious! Sieves to be squeezed through, fornication through chain-link and other walls we must ingest. But just how pointed are your teeth? We find out by turning our intent inward – and the sharper our spit-shine bone the less it will hurt. The blood only mirrors our enthusiasm as it bursts out of its coop!

And who could blame us? Especially as children! Feeling the grip of a doomed, already trudged and unimagined future around our necks, where the more we dig up, the more we want to either hide, bear arms, or slowly kill ourselves! As the most instinctive form of protest against this rising tide, it begins first with the unquenchable need to feel good by any and all means necessary. The means in question was the only tradition we championed. We pass the torch. Fire that makes the lights go out! Those inclined to scoff should instead rest easy, knowing that people like us were never trying to communicate with you.

Whether we were the offspring of sordid town rummies or the spawn of sober New Agers was inconsequential. Our backgrounds are mere scenery and have little to do with where and how we spend our time. While there was some irreparable tragedy dished out in equal portions to all of us, in the grand panorama this had no bearing on the trigger-fingers of our idle hands – sprinkles on the big black cake.

We'd curse the automaton world swearing never to follow orders blindly, but more than most we were guilty of living like Pavlov's dogs. Especially when night fell – this, our inverted signal, the vast burnt out bulb, would make us scurry like roaches to the liquor stores, then to the beaches or parks, if our Queen Bee – our emaciated, enabling Den Mother – had gotten too unruly back at our second home.

Once enough of us had gathered you couldn't really call it just drinking. Every night was a new challenge of mental and physical endurance, far removed from any frat-house trappings. In fact, I believe your cringing would contort into entirely new directions, pointing to ways more profoundly masochistic and emotionally vomiteering. Everyone engaged, everyone reacting, everyone affected. Unconsciously constructing a world far beyond the splaying of guts and forgetting of inhibitions. This was a perpetual, self-contained circus of the willfully damned. Draining every last bottle as fast as we could, as if it were a race. If you didn't take that sip, someone else would grab your bottle and beat you to it. We were fighting each other bare fisted, administering fresh razor blades to our eager skin in semi-private moments, screaming Satan's name in painful grating wails, breaking bottles, plotting detailed, fool-proof murders of certain people the world would hopefully forget about. We stripped naked on the edges of cliffs, burnt small animals to death. Triple-vision swimming to the horizon to escape seaweed hogties. Rooftop circle jerking. Breaking vein virginities. Shooting out car windows with BB guns. Hallucinating human oddities silently judging us in the trees. Blind-riding paramedic chariots. Snorting brown and green amphetamines making the night not only longer, but faster. Playing chicken in our 100mph clown-cars in the wrong lane. Frantic public fornication with any briefly requited crush until we realized we had fallen victim to every chemical naturally occurring inside our brain, under the sun or the kitchen sink. Then, girl gangs were formed to rough up outsider bitches and the guys began to suck each other off.

Where else could we go was hardly the question, but just *how many times* could we go, back to the store in one night? Two o'clock had nothing on us, as we still had hands at this point. There was no sating until vision itself had ceased.

Only a fool would claim this wasn't out of love – our collective compulsion to grab each other by the hair, to dunk our heads into the liquid, then pull back to re-emerge just seconds before the bubbles rise. And if not love, then it is born from the unwavering encouragement to expand these prison walls. If we didn't care, we would instead stay dry, to collect dust and be forgotten.

But there are assured moments of absolute precariousness where we might bear witness to the initial conception of those bubbles, much of their wonderment derived from the large chance that these flashes of the bottomless abyss, where the only way to the other side is across this sort of slack-heavy tightrope, the goal in and of itself.

PART
THREE

ONE

I wasn't entirely sure why I insisted on keeping the car windows rolled up tight in 102 degree weather on the way to my appointment. I had no AC, and I was sweating my latest bender out profusely, so I justified this self-administered torture as a poor man's sauna detox. When I got to rapid panting, I would start to roll the window down, only to quickly roll it back up when the sour exhaust of a hundred other cars began to creep into mine. Los Angeles traffic creates its own interstellar microclimate, what one would think the uninhabitable, gaseous air of Venus may be akin to. I simply required all the armor around me I could get, as I never felt more vulnerable. I was afraid of myself, for myself, and for others, from myself.

Six pm wasn't odd for this kind of bumper to bumper on Hollywood Blvd., but the sluggish procession hadn't moved in almost ten minutes. I rolled down my window only to stick my head out to see if there was construction going down somewhere down the line of idling vehicles. There were no hardhats or noise of invasive machinery. What I saw was more unsettling. Hundreds of people locking arms, in what appeared to be a demonstration of sorts, quickly unfolding in the middle of the boulevard. I saw the human chain coming down the median and swiftly continuing to form past my car, where I was nearly able to get a better look. They all wore the same T-shirt but I was too panic-stricken to read the words emblazoned. I kept whipping my drenched head around, wondering if they would ever let us through. They were not aggressive – some had their heads down in prayer, reflection, or shame. Others just stared deadpan brave into the ever-obstructed horizon as if to tell the world to bring it. I rolled up my window, down my window, and up again.

It finally dawned on me that I was smack dab in Little Armenia, once I saw the banner unfolding across the side of my car. It was the annual Armenian Genocide protest, to raise awareness of the unprovoked rape, slaughter, and robbing of their whole culture's humble footprint by the Turks. My orphaned synapses quivered like worms after rain, struggling to conjoin, creating a friction as if my whole head was on fire. I pondered my own Irish in their plight, where at our worst we became alcoholic terrorists who would orchestrate home invasion assassinations of whole families just for knowing a cousin of a cousin of our vague English oppressors from decades ago. But I was defeated in my attempted empathy once I read the rest of their t-shirt: NEVER FORGET. Fuck my own vaguely oppressed culture - the problem with me is that not only could I never remember, I was also both the oppressed and the oppressor in my own personal apocalypse. Plus, I was late to my first appointment with this Dr. James Waiken character, to try to get to the bottom of this hole. Little did I know that with a hole this twisted and turned, as we would try to shine a light down into it, more shadows would form, shifting tauntingly with each moving illumination.

James was referred to me by my ex-girlfriend Cecilia. I trust her judgment only on account that she might even know my condition better than I do, as not just a spectator but also an occasional unwilling participant. While her and I no longer speak, she implored me to get in touch with him during one of our last talks. I felt I had no argument against trying everything. She spoke highly of the man - after all, he made her feel so comfortable she decided to go ahead and fuck him during one of their very first sessions, a mere two days after we split up. "Hell," I thought, "if I drove her to the point of seeking therapy that quickly, perhaps I should indulge and follow suit with comparable urgency…"

I finally arrive at Dr. James Waiken's office above the old bank building on Spring and 6th. I pay too much to park and find the ground level, leading me to four long flights of marbled stairs.

I find his office after walking the length of the hallway, room 247 on the left. I ring the doorbell. I ring it again. James opens the door on my third attempt, as if I decoded my entry. "You must be Caleb!" he says with an over-confident grin. I reach out my hand to meet his. "That is right. Pleasure, Dr. Waiken."

"Well, business first... Why don't you have a seat?" he said, arm outstretched to his black leather couch under a wide, tall window overlooking downtown, one of the many focal points of in his illustrious office.

I obliged, though feeling out of place in a room so sophisticated.

"So," James started in, "I know a little about you from what Cecilia has told me and from your and I's brief introduction on the phone, but I'd love to hear your concerns and what you would like to get out of this session in your own words, so we can proceed clearly."

"Well, it's hard to know where to begin. I have done damage to myself, to others, and *from* others, to my inners, and my outers... but it doesn't feel like it's me that is responsible."

"I'll say!" James cheekily replied, "That doesn't sound very responsible at all!"

"Uh, no. I mean, I am convinced that the scenarios are so out of control, but pinpointing, that there's some other force. My hands, not my brain. Not my soul. Why would I want to hurt anyone?"

"Just add alcohol. That active ingredient, right?"

"Uh, yes... to a degree. That's the lubrication for this, uh, entry into my will. The kindling for the fire, but not the match. Not the will to burn anything in its path."

"Do you feel possessed? Can we use that word?"

"Yes. Please."

"Well, " James continued, "there is a lot of history with the correlations between alcohol and spirit possession. Oddly enough, there's not been a single book written on the subject, but if you research each subject on its own, the similar characteristics are staggering. But you know, this would be considered pseudo-science, and it doesn't really hold water among my colleagues."

"I get it. You're the professional. But as someone who falls victim to alcoholic blackouts, I'd like it if we could focus on the profundity of this phenomenon, leave science out of it - the blackout."

"Sure, go ahead and take the floor, Caleb."

I took his cue quite literally, and got up off the couch and began to pace.

"It's like a complete surrender of mind, body and soul to a greater force. The stuff religion is made of, but not from a benevolent God..."

James interrupted, "Oh sure, I mean the history of wine and religion goes back to thousands..."

"No, hold on... please. Just let me talk for a while! Ok? I can't lose this train of thought."

"My bad, Caleb. Go ahead."

"It's far more primitive than religion. Like a toxic walkabout to where our consciousness sidewalk leads to a cliff's edge, where we leap with an eager, running start, our pride falling past us, faster than we could catch up with. It's transcendence of intention. A blind glimpse into an invisible world where any number of disembodied entities can have their way with us, the way children handle rag dolls. It's an out-of-body experience. So enveloping that we can only really submit to the second party's external account of the experience, rather than our own internal vision shackled in paradox."

"Okay." James intervened, "Let's focus on the brain for a moment. Are you familiar with the Medial Temporal Lobes?"

I nodded my head politely, allowing him to continue.

"The MTL are where both our episodic, you know, *autobiographical* events, as well as our declarative memories are stored. Cruelly, this is also where alcoholic excess prefers to make its most elusive marks. Erasure. Now, this is also the part of the brain that operates the rollercoasters of trauma, audio hallucinations, and epilepsy. Before the age of prescription drugs, the MTL would actually be removed altogether from epileptics to eliminate seizures. Basic motor skills would remain intact, as well as the storage of short-term memory, so long as the triggering remained undistracted. Now, the primary side effect of this primitive therapy was that it would render patients unable to form new memories, even out of the most standout facts and events. So, for those of us – and I admit, I am one too – who find ourselves in the constant throes of playing catch up with our alcoholic antics, this should send shivers to us, once we see the correlation between medicine's ignorant, almost sadistic past, and our own masochistic flooding of our precious cells with what is essentially a potential poison."

"Wait, ok... back up. You're a bit, uh, *touched* by the spirits too?" I asked.

"Scotch," said James, frankly, "imagine what I do all day and dare to think I can actually sleep at night without having to obliterate my brain a bit? Who's gonna shrink the head of the head shrinker? Scotch. One cell at a time."

I smiled. Some common ground was beginning to reveal itself.

James continued with a humble laugh, "Think about it. I see about six to eight clients a day. I commit myself to them so deeply that by the end of that day, I feel like I need be committed. All those desperate voices floating in my head when I am finally alone. I feel schizophrenic. But I am a professional. Most professionals will drink their day faces off in their spare time. It's just rare that they would admit it, especially to a client. But this is the subject, right?"

I nodded my head.

"That's the difference between my colleagues and I – I would never demonize alcohol. If we are in touch with the balance of nature and possess the profundity of birth, death, and re-birth, then what could be more akin than our own imbibing? It splays itself out as one accurate essence of not only comfortably inhabiting, but escaping our imperfect soul."

"The intertwining of sex and death." I agreed.

"Scary, but well put. I had this thought earlier, let me grab this book…" James said as he walked over to his mahogany bookcase, "*Religion and Wine* by Robert C. Fuller." He showed me the non-descript magenta cover. "Fuller unfolds the mystic influence of our world's most beloved crushed grape staple, exuding a wisdom that could easily apply to all forms of alcohol in less formal but still *ritualistic* settings, like you and I are used to. 'There is no other drink like it known to humanity,'" James recited out of the pages. "'Only wine is used as a sacramental drink. In fact, wine is like the incarnation – it is both divine and human.' He further muses on the laborious process of growing the grapes, to the fermentation, to the storage and aging as the perfect cooperation of God's gifts – Earth, water, sun – resulting in a scared tonic that induces a euphoric lightness that seems to bridge the gap between Man and God. It's a humble surrender."

James wouldn't stop talking, "Catholicism helped kick-start this connection, using wine as a symbol for God's blessing, a gift to enjoy a *gladdening of the heart* while in turn, rather morbidly signifying the Blood that Christ gushed out of his wounds…"

"As if we are actually eagerly catching his blood with our chalices, right?" I interjected.

"Right," James concurred, "it is still believed, that by enjoying a sip, that you are virtually surrendering yourself to the spirit of the Holy Ghost."

"OK!" I threw my palms up in frustrated presentation, "So, you are saying there is reason to believe there may be other, more savage entities passing through you as well? Why wouldn't they? Especially considering the advent of Jesus helped create the concept of evil as its counterpart?"

James thought for a moment. "Well, the undercurrent of intoxicants seems to sever ties of the human spirit from the restrictive confines of the mind and body. We've seen other people witness this in awe, as drunkenness often causes nailed down logic to be turned on its head... Perhaps suggesting the possibility that something otherworldly is occurring. It rides a thin line between mysticism and conventional, every day ritual. This line must be blurred in order to have a true understanding, that while we are drinking with these insatiable appetites, we may also be communing with elements other than our own flesh and blood."

There was silence.

"Fuck it!" James got up from his seat.

"What?" I asked.

"Let's go get a drink," he said, grabbing his cord blazer.

While this felt absolutely *naughty*, James assured me on the way downstairs to the bar that this wasn't really out of the ordinary for him, a psychologist who pays the bills by day listening to people cry about their molestations, neglects, depressions and projections. To these patients he nods neutrally, occasionally interjecting some vague, uncommitted opinions before smoothly turning them 180 degrees, creating a vast contradictory landscape of their shattered lives in which they somehow walk away from refreshed and reassured.

"Most of the time," he said, "I have not said anything helpful or for that matter even coherent. They could be talking to the pizza man on the other end of a phone and probably get similar results!"

This is not to imply that James is in any way a man without merit, nor by any means a hack taking advantage of the vulnerability of others. He has merely been at it far too long, and has by default found an effortless way to coast through the more mind-numbing moments of his profession. He actually sees himself as over-qualified for the job, with not nearly enough opportunity to explore the more abnormal paths of the human condition he had hoped for earlier in his career.

To fill this void of monotony, James has gradually created a more excavating, adventurous underside to his field of expertise that could only exist off the record – mainly for fear of his hypercritical colleagues spreading rumors and putting his reputation at stake. On private recommendations only, and for which these nocturnal patients don't pay a dime, James will organize more erect, couch-less meetings in semi-private environments. Usually a bar with a secluded backroom, where inhibition's wheels can truly be greased, where a steady intake of alcohol is only broken by exploding epiphany, where the roles of doctor and patient are blurred from the inherent wisdom of the mutual slur. James usually finds one of these sessions to be more enlightening than all ten years of his daylight whiners combined, often times shedding light on his own unquenchable thirst for scotch, in particular. But for James it is not just any rotting alcoholic who has no control over his own actions leaving a trail of destruction from motives unknown that will really do.

"I guess I just know it when I see it," he tells me.,"a couple years ago, I had this patient who seemed beyond help, completely unwilling to cooperate, so much so that I wondered why he bothered to visit, much less pay me; but for some reason he did have the cash to burn while managing to be one of the most vengeful, dysfunctional winos I've ever had the displeasure to console. He had completely given up, lost everything including any kind of emotional foundation for us to build upon. Even his face had started to fall apart - you know what I'm talking about? When your liver gets so backed up it starts pushing all the toxic blood into your face and slowly collapses under its own weight? Anyway, our sessions consisted of me trying inquisitively to sculpt some kind of human being under all this and him vaguely mumbling when he wasn't silently staring at the window. So, as you can imagine, after two sessions a week for a month, even a professional has a tipping point, right? I needed a drink and couldn't care less about any arbitrary code of ethics. So instead of adjourning the session, I took him downstairs to the bar - my contrarian side taking over - and we continued the session there. I even sprung for the straight vodka he wanted – probably one of the most irresponsible things a guy like me could do, on many a level. But what do you know? We sat down and he opened right up! He was talking more than me at one point. I realized that with some types, especially alcoholics, you have to get past the stigma of their vice just to get them talking. Get them out of that classic paralysis that occurs when there's a looming element of judgment and guilt involved in a situation that should be open-ended and in most instances, unpredictable with the results."

TWO

There we sat, in the backroom of Cole's in the throes of a botched downtown remodel. Stained-glass windows offered no more clarity to the outside world than in that wretched church. We were there to travel inward, using four walls closing in on us to squeeze every last drop of precious oil out of our stubborn synapses. I spilled my guts, along with my second neat scotch, wiping it up with the tail of my trench coat. We have been here for about an hour, drinking slow, for now.

He chimes in after a long silence, letting the climax of my story of teenage possession settle in a bit.

"So, the obvious Devil's advocate, or rather hung jury decision, is that half the people you would tell this story to would think you were full of shit. They would consider you no more than blacked-out drunk, not remembering all the atrocious things you did as you grasp for the absurd scapegoat of spirit possession in an effort to rid yourself of any guilt. Correct?"

"Well," I half laughed, "No, not really! You might think so, given the outlandishness of the story, but I can say in all confidence that almost everyone I have relayed this to stay silent and attentive, unwilling to debate! They all say that the thought has crossed their mind before, if not from a first hand experience, then from someone very close to them who's very literally turned into a fucking monster…"

James interrupted, "Oh no, I know! Believe me, I am not necessarily trying to contest your claims! For your sake, I am trying to whittle it down. For skepticism's sake. You can't say 'I am possessed by evil spirits summoned by excessive alcohol consumption' and just expect that to be the grand thesis! If that were the case, then both sides of the spectrum, whether they believed you or not, would agree that you were nuts and just leave it at that without further exploration!"

"Well, being nuts in this case shouldn't be confused with the validity of possession. I have been told I am crazy all of my life. Not for a fucking second has it made me doubt myself! I have been forced to accept it!!!" I could tell by his slight recoil that my volume had increased.

"Good. Like I was saying, I want to strip this notion until we are seeing eye to eye on something indisputable from any outsider's perspective, got it?"

I nodded in solemn agreement. I noticed a slight decline in his eloquence combined with an acute determination in his emphasis on certain climactic syllables. He continued, "There is a lot I can tell you with my own experiences with this, but I want to wait until it's more appropriate, or rather maybe comes out more spontaneous..."

"Sure..." I replied, almost as a question.

"Now, I think it's safe to say that we're both smart enough to know that there's no such thing as the Devil or Satan or demons – not in the traditional Hollywood or Christian Church sense where it's an actual embodiment or entity that you can just get rid of through exorcism or incessant praying."

"Right, of course. But that said, when I talk of possession I am referring to the same thing as they are. The Christians, for example. The downfall with their version comes from their fear of the unknown, which, in order to gain some kind of prehistoric control over it, they give it a name, a face, and lines are drawn of between good and evil, a bloody, ignorant war is declared – no mention that their whole institution's foundation and definition of enlightenment is to be possessed by a spirit and so... Listen, let's not lead this into some dorm room discussion of theology. You get my point though."

James nodded with a heavy brow and let me continue.

"The people that were there that night, they don't even feel comfortable talking about it. They go white. When they do talk, they all say the same thing – that if I was blacked out, in the traditional alcohol induced sense, there's no way I could have been carrying myself with that kind of determined lucidity. Sure, I was speaking some kind of tongue but I was something else, only limited by my frame. Something about that night, whenever it's brought up, seems to whisk people right back to that static hour and they prefer not to discuss. There was something disarming, beyond drunken violence... You know, it's hardly even my argument you understand, but more so the witnesses. If this were a trial, I'd be shrugging my shoulders, merely having to just throw my arms up and point to those who were there! But the verdict is pointless in a way – there is no punishment anyone can dish out, I have to *live* with this condition."

"So, you are saying that on this night you were, and continue to be, a vessel for a certain *ill Spirit*, but not a demon, not the Devil, nor anything you can give a name or a face to... a Spirit though, one that removes you from your consciousness, using you for its own destructive intentions, your flesh the vehicle... Sounds like classic demon possession to me!" he said.

At this point I could not tell if the man was fucking with me, merely batting me around like cat would with a half-dead mouse. I interjected, "Okay. AGAIN, listen! I do not believe in the fucking Devil or any of his demons anymore than I believe in God. What I do believe is that man is capable of creating environments that can embody, create a certain *Spirit*, that could form a tension so thick that in turn can touch you, penetrate you, and depending on your will, potentially take you over!"

"Okay," he said, satisfied, "now we're getting somewhere. Go on, please."

"Okay. For example, do you ever walk into a hotel room and

become instantly stifled, overpowered by the accumulative force of emotional residue? It stops you in your tracks. You're ambiguously conflicted. You don't know whether to break down in tears or strangle the nearest neck! Either way you feel somehow altered, dizzy. The air seems to fluctuate in consistency."

"Oh sure, sure. And the sort of unsettling lucid dreaming that always seems to follow? I have had nights in hotels where the dreams were so vivid I am not sure if I had really slept." He paused. "I think this occurs from environments that are transient in nature. The more lives that pass through the threshold, the larger the scope of... well, I guess what we are now calling possession."

A genuine momentum was entering our conversation and perhaps I was even finding a kindred spirit in this fucking hack.

I ordered another Rusty Nail.

"Right." I concurred, "All these ghost and demon terminologies, as quaint and evocative as they are, they're really just a sense of folklore overstaying its welcome and creating a certain ignorance around something very obvious and strange, in the same way we used to think the Earth was flat. While it is a theory that has since rendered itself obsolete, the fact that we know the Earth is round is also begs further questions regarding what else is around us."

"Now, let me ask you," he continued, "Before this whole night, previous to moving into this tainted apartment, had you ever had any similar experiences? You were obviously well steeped in alcoholic excess before this. I think with an alcoholic slant to our thesis, it'd be foolish to think that incident would have been the first time."

I giggled mischievously, "I remember blacking out for the first time when I was about seventeen, mind you I was already about three to four years into this," I said, raising my glass, "While most kids were sippin' Slurpees, we had already done everything, alcohol remaining the preferred constant. Daily maintenance! So, seventeen, there was a big wino shindigger at 461 High Dr. It was Big Jim's getting-out-of-jail-welcome-home party. Got a fancy keg of Budweiser. I swear I drank half that thing to myself, trying to outdo, if not just keep up with the older seasoned winos, who were all howling, rolling on the ground, pissing their pants and what not. Again, this was an older crowd, all of these salt-water Skid Row types that somehow became shadowy presences to our teenage lives, spending every day on the beach drinking with them, mainly because we were all trying to get somewhere else but just couldn't make it past the ocean."

James roared with laughter, decibels almost drowning out my raised tone, "Okay, okay, cut to the chase! Where's the lights out?"

"All right, so my last memory of the evening is this senior citizen sagging tit walking wrinkle named Freddie – a woman, if you could call it that. Ended up moving away to Texas and pulling a train with some skinheads, but whatever… Anyway, she walks into the garage where we all were, wearing nothing but a black lace teddy. Freddie in a teddy, right? With an acoustic guitar strapped to her she comes in and serenades us…"

I stood on the table to channel Freddie.

"It's so sad
When the one
You love is dead."

(First, a gentle strum with each line sentimentally whispered.)

"It's so sad
When the one
You love
Is dead."

(This went on for an uncomfortable, but highly anticipatory five minutes, until the deadly refrain of…)

"Oh it's so sad…
OH IT'S SO SAD!!!
IT'S SO FUCKING SAD!!!
IT'S… SO… FUCKING… SAAAAAAAAD!!!!"

"She started growling in a Cookie Monster voice in all of our faces, strumming violently in hyper sixteenths. The crowd roared applause, whistles, and laughter. I remember one of her tits hanging out when she was done and then... lights out. I woke up on the beach the next afternoon, losing about fourteen hours of re-collective history. Apparently through the course of the evening, I was going up to everyone in a panic, shaking their shoulders while pointing up, saying, 'They're still up in the trees! They're still watching us!!!' before burying myself with anything I could find – cans, bottles, newspaper, dirt. At one point I began digging a very large hole in the weed garden, most likely for myself."

James smiled sympathetically, "As bright as it can make the world, I've also found alcohol to have a tendency to give us a doomed third eye, washing the most harmless situations with a tee-tering-on-the-edge-of-the-world hue. It can bring us out of the deepest depression and suddenly make the whole world come to life, but with that sometimes the *whole* world does *actually* come alive – the invisible, the inanimate..."

I excitedly cut him off, "No doubt. I am convinced it blurs worlds, dimensions. When I was still with Cecilia, there was this one night where I was having one of my frequent episodes. After hours of me thrashing about, she finally allowed me to have my last drink of the night. I was begging for it. I knew I was too far-gone and had to knock out. I faded. She got me to bed, but within about five minutes I woke up screaming at the walls. I had bought her an amazing antique bellows the previous Christmas, all rusted turquoise with a pirate ship engraved into its teardrop shape. It hung on the wall directly in front of our bed. I woke up alone, shaking, going through some kind of DTs, the bellows being the first thing I saw. Though instead of perceiving it as the bellows, my submerged mind saw it as a taunting, animated, old-timey, bloated pear-shaped tax man caricature – you know, with the suit, mustache, and top hat –

coming straight for me, morphing into hundreds of tax men from the original bellows, as if looking through a hall of mirrors, and every time I moved, he and his single file army would gain on me. It was clear to me that this man was the harbinger of my own personal apocalypse! With a shriek I ordered him back into the wall. I think Cecilia burst in the door while I was standing on the bed screaming 'NO! NO! NO!' I was trying to overpower this thing just by pointing at it."

James cracked another smile from behind the hand covering half his face, "Yeah, well all bets are off at that point, right? When someone is faced with hallucinations, or okay, *Spirits* so real that it creates tangible emotional and physical waves within and outside of a person, then what does it truly matter whether it is *real* or not? Again, a person's subjective reality has been turned on its head. It *is* real. Cecilia is lucky all you did was point at the thing and holler a bit. If it was me I would have shattered everything that wasn't nailed down."

I laughed, "Well sadly I've done that too. I didn't even know what a commemorative plate was until I came of a blackout with her screaming I had just smashed one to bits. If I am going crazy then I usually make sure everything is coming with me."

My mind momentarily wandered the gamut of irrevocable remorse, a silent eruption quickly extinguished by a catatonic haze, where thoughts go to die. I wandered privately to another instance I had been trying to reconcile ever since it occurred. Being dragged out of my apartment with a bloody fat lip and loose tooth gifted to me by her fucking hero friend that had no idea what was really going on. It's not as if you can hear a girl screaming at the top of her lungs from outside then when you bust through the door all you find in the house is that girl on the ground crying. Me on the bed in a fetal position not knowing where I was, who I was and him, thinking he's got the right to break my face. This could have been the same night I was wandering by myself in the backyard peering through our neighbor's window mumbling that I was trying to bury their teeth in the ground.

Coming to, I shamefully realized James had been talking for a while now.

"Hey, you there still?"

"Sorry, yeah. Just had that fateful sip, you know?"

"Sure. How far back should I start over?"

Brick faced, I shrugged.

"Well, I was just saying we could easily compare our own over-indulgence in drinking alcohol to the mystic who has abused his own powers. When we have been given this gift, one of conscious-ness-lifting, bliss-filling wonderment, it is our tendency to embrace it until·it becomes a two-way stranglehold, taking for granted its ef-fects, wanting to fill every inch of our being with as much of the li-quid as we can afford or find, rather than the residual benefits and uninhibited channels it gracefully opens. You see, we deceive ourselves trying to 'get there' rather than bearing witness to the serenity. Then, the next thing you know we have sped past our des-tination. Born from our grand conflict with duality, it should be our gospel to do anything in our power to have alcohol retain its rever-ence!"

I dozed off for a few seconds and woke up to his...

"Touching on the whole Dionysian concept. Its popular reputa-tion is one of complete indulgent revelry. Bottomless pleasure by any means necessary. But in view of its full spectrum, there is a large element of masochism involved in this philosophy. The conscious gravitation towards the kind of pain overindulgence brings..."

I half-consciously nodded with my fist shoved in my face for support.

"Now, we all know this fine line. We are so familiar with the split of the two sides, that we can't tell them apart. The realm of Dionysus is also a realm where truth and illusion happen simultaneously, and true, TRUE, TRUE madness only occurs when we insist on separating the two."

His eyes went tidal with every escalating mention of the word *true*. I took a stealth comfort in catching a couple slurs in his speech. The alcohol was slowly but surely chipping away at his stiff, professional elegance.

He continued, "Now, we must lay to waste everything we have ever been told about alcohol – every last reactionary report, every cautionary tale, every inflated advertisement emphasizing everything *but* its actual inherent alchemic - if not nightmarish - wonder. We must realize that we have been criminally misled, and once we see this, then we must take an even farther-out view of what is actually happening from the time the insatiable craving hits, to the stumbling zombie walk all the way past our house and into the trees.

"Admit it. We drink because we are trying to reach the goal of oblivion. We have been shackled and beaten by the tyranny of routine, left with some shreds of dignity, holding an unquenchable desire for something not of this rigid world. To turn this world inside out. So here we are. Drinking with great fervor, yes. Smiling, crying, and yes, killing our brain cells. But perhaps these casualties are cells we simply no longer have any use for? We can see this act as one of emotional, and physical inventory. We forget that expansion must happen by decay just as well as any pro-active efforts. Wallowing in the dirt can also be like gardening, in a way..."

His analogy woke me up a bit. I knew James was preaching the truth but he was also clinically boring me to snores. I threw more kerosene on this gratuitous grease-fire and got us two neat scotches, wanting more than anything to feel that specific punch to the brain that was eluding me thus far. This conversation was only scratching the surface. No doubt we were getting *somewhere*, agreeing on most points, but it wasn't exactly the kind of hard truth I was necessarily looking for. Perhaps by its very nature, it was more *liquid.*

I drooled while he prattled. Then I raised a toast, which he thoughtfully interrupted.

"Cheers, James! I wanted to just…"

"Enthusiasmos!" he replied, implying our drinks.

"What's that now?"

"It's Latin for 'possession by God."

"Oh, cute," I said, "alrighty, then. ENTHUSIASMOS!"

Clink!

"Anyway," I went on, "this gravitation towards self-destruction is a natural thing, a way of excavating our core, displaying our soul, etc… I'm sorry but this does not make my condition any easier to handle. I am overqualified, well versed in willful disintegration, and with that I find certain comfort in being taken to the brink of death so I emerge victorious, beating my chest! What I go through is anything but willful!!! You can talk all you want about the birth and death cycle, the mistry of mazochism, fffugging Dionysus…"

It was around this time that things started to get blurry. I believe James cut me off at "fucking Dionysus." An argument ensued. I remember his eyes getting real big. This had to have been our sixth cocktail in our third hour there. We were drinking slowly until this point. The bartender came to the table to scold us about our obscene volume, despite the fact that we were the only ones left in the back room. It was also 1:56am and they had already announced last call, much to our highly involved ignorance. James took the barkeep aside for what seemed like an eternity. I rolled each remaining ice cube around in my mouth until it melted, not wanting to waste even a molecule of scotch.

Whatever it was he told the bartender, James returned smiling, four beautifully sweating Rusty Nails in hand, holding them precari-

ously in a diamond formation. The bartender followed not far behind, and also came to our table smiling, letting us know that he was
locking the door behind him and that we were welcome to stay as
long as we wanted, pointing to the back door, which would auto-
matically lock behind us whenever we decided to spill into the alley.
An impressive performance by James, whatever psychic vampirism
he used to seduce him with - most likely money - granting us free
reign over this alcoholic antechamber for the night! The euphoria of
good fortune was quickly diffused with panic however, as I
wondered if these four Rusty Nails would be enough.

"Pishin' for b'ol, Janes?"

He grinned, digging in his pockets and slipping a fifty-spot from
his money clip, "This gonbee one long night I'm frayed."

The bartender rolled his eyes all the way back to the bar, pro-
pelled only by his heavy sighs. He returned with a bottle of Tullamore Dew and a bucket of ice, a towering display on the table.

"Have a long night, fellas." The bartender grinned reluctantly,
walking out the door with a reverberating clang of the lock, an
echoing choke of finality.

I vaguely remember taking each drained tumbler glass and
chucking the remaining ice against the wall. I lined them up, all
fourteen or fifteen around the edge of the round table, starting with
four on each corner as if they were the 12, 3, 6, and 9 on the clock.

I pointed to each one.

"Noorht, Soth, Ees, West! This izn caze we gelostagin."

James guffawed. I continued, placing the rest of other glasses in
between these primary four.

"Kay, now whas that?" he asked as I was gingerly picking up the
table and rotating it ninety degrees.

"NOW! WE ARE LOST! ENTHUSIASMOS!!!" I screamed,
overturning the ice bucket, successfully filling each glass and any
other thirsty surface besides.

James laughed like an automatic weapon, "'L'ow me! Eelow, me please!" he blurted out, taking the bottle of Tullamore and filling the glasses, one flooding pour in multiple revolutions around the table. We both stood up as if rehearsed, stumbled pirouettes around the scene, each quickly draining a glass while sloppily toasting with the empties.

"ENTHUSIASMOS!!!"

"ENTHUSIASMOS!!!"

...but this time with such a fucked-off force we shattered the tumblers right into our hands, fresh-born shards entered flesh, blood mingled with the whiskey, ice dripped off our palms as protruding, serrated foundations hit the table with clumsy bangs. I could feel a pulse in my palm, forcing the blood out of the incredible gash from the web of my pinky to the fleshy part below my thumb. We laughed ourselves out of breath as I put my mutilated hand over my heart in an arcane gesture, finding some relief that my heart was beating in the same rhythm as the blood pumping out of my hand. The vitals were still connected, therefore everything was going to be okay. James's hand looked far worse - he didn't seem to mind as he grabbed another drink off the table. The displacement of all the whiskey glasses looked like some evacuated black magic ritual gone completely awry, little droplets forming pools of blood over ice and golden brown glistening diamond-slush. Lights from the ceiling illuminating each glass like abandoned candles in a once calculated formation.

We let the rigor mortis of our little outburst set in as we sat back down, verbalizing our exhalation.

"Uhhhhhhaaahhh..."

"Yeah, James er great buhidint cum heer to talktua buk. Any chance we cud tok like we jus danced? Yooo tol me erlier yo-ad yer own speriense withis shit anal yoanna say is about the rorld. Thiz doz]nt have AYTHING todo with this rarld! Whengyoo git molsted by the *Spurts*?!?"

"Fuck man yud be pain me to tok laka buk! Maybe you're nod even lizenin' this 'ol time! Your passin out erlier… gimmy break!!! You get drunk you blakote, but before you do, yousey shadows clowzin in first? Like they mayey shount beether? Losta lite but stull shadows, yeah?"

"I seein 'em ry now asshole, all over yer fuggin face!"

"Wull thoz shadows are jus you looginina meer. Isyer dark flip-side fuggin shadow self! Yer bout to blakote prolllly and yunowit these shadows ga tayk up yer hol vision soon."

"Fucking HELL! Yer jus regurgitating Carl Jung or Freud ina my moth ligim a fuggin baby bird arntchu? You don getit, I've fuggin flown man! Buh I fly incirgles! I paz on the carrion and prey straight on things thastill knowata live and love! Now THAZ the problem! See theez hans!?! They're neot connacted to ayone buh me buh I cat saya same fer my brain! I catevin say this is my blood ay mor!!!"

I pointed to the gloopy geyser coming out of my annihilated hand. I think I got up and poured the remains of the bottle in two glasses that weren't quite shattered yet but when I took a sip there were crunchy things that wouldn't really melt. We sat in silence, sipping, chewing, spitting, and staring at one another in mutual dripping intimidation. He was slowly dissolving into three of himself in my fortified vision, subtly overlapping the mouth that broke the muted chill.

"Alrite, my turn kay?"

"Good. GO! Bout time!"

"Well, thirs a lomore reesins why we're both here than you my think. Yer obiusly fruserated rhynow an maybe weneeya change the terms of thiz meeting a bit, maybe considir it more ova playdate then counseling."

"Whatha fuckarya evn talggin bout?!?!"

"Heh… She said we dserved eash other." He paused, "You really don't know whatadituwer, do you? To Cecilia?"

"No!" My face went flush, "Nope! Sure don't!"

"Well, get comfy… use this too, yer bleedin outtayer mouth." He said as he handed me the least of the whiskey soaked napkins.

"Kay fer Chrissakes go head!"

"All right… so, we met thrua mutual fren thawas tryna helper…"

"I DON'T WANT YOUR LIFE STORY!!! WHO IS THE FUGGIN SHRINK HERE!?!?" I screamed as I hurled a glass right past his head. "WHAT DID YOU DO TO HER!!!"

He was the only person in my whole life to ever refrain from even flinching from my aggressive offences, which only fanned the flames.

He steadied his speech the best he could. "Well, you know our first session together quickly evolved into a sort of date…"

"Yes, yes I fugging know!"

I knew but this moment somehow had all the raw surprise of hearing it for the first time.

"Or so I thought! You're obviously no stranger to gray areas so hopefully you understand this."

"LIZZIN!! HOBOUT don't worry if I understand. Talk!"

Collective adrenaline had leveled out our slurs for a moment, as we submitted into disintegration. One more moment of exhausted silence, where we looked behind us on the path which we came only to be met with an enveloping uncertainty. James dripped out a slow-motion stutter.

"She walked into my office rather wide-eyed, looking around… You seen my office, but is really iz fancy! People comment on it quite frequently. Especially the huge twenty by ten foot window with the view of downtown, which she promptly positioned herself right in front of. So you can imagine, lots of light coming through that window at three in the afternoon, and… let's just say I appreciated the vantage."

"What… the fuck… are you trying to tell me?" I asked glaringly.

I knew what he was trying to tell me. I remembered her extreme aversion to wearing underwear, refusing to adorn her midsection, almost as rule – she claimed that even underneath her clothes, they had the *inherent lock of chastity*. I always got such a kick out of this lovely quirk until this very second. Familiar sensations began to boil inside me, causing my sight to get spotty and a numbness slowly disconnecting me from my actions.

"I think you know what I am trying to tell you! What else would make me lose focus on the appointment!?!"

The words fell from my mouth like the runs, "I KNOW THAT CUNT LIKE THE PALM OF MY HAND!!! WHAT ELSE!?!"

James put it his head down in shame only to put it right back up rolling his eyes, "She was looking at me like I knew, we both knew! Then I asked her if she wanted ice water or scotch. SHE SAID SCOTCH!!!"

"THAT'S CAUSE SHE'S VURY SPEZIFIGALLY A FUCK-ING BOOZEHOUND NOT A FUCKING WHORE!!!"

James was cowering silently, slowly dangling his head.

"AND THEN?!?!"

I hurled another glass, aiming for that stupid buoying head but instead hitting his Adam's apple. He grasped his neck with both hands trying to gasp for air, hissing out some facsimile of "Please! Stop! Please settle down... PLEASE!" A lot of pathetic *pleases*. He finally   regained   his   inhalation   after   a   loud "BUUUUUUURRRRP!!!"

"Listen, I cannot continue with this these kind of reactions! I haven't really told you much and now I am not even sure I can..."

And with that, already white-knuckling our table, my fingers sent the whole shattered scene right into his face, then lap, before swiftly throwing him backwards in his chair as he tried to scramble away. I stood teetering, half-blind, already wondering what had happened, why James was frantically crawling on the floor like a hog on ice towards the door. I made an instant automaton advance towards him. I rejoiced in what convenient handles his lapels were as I grabbed them, almost yanking his coat clear off – my right hand still burning, unable to close from its self-administered stigmata. With James in tow, I scurried in reverse, dragging him back to our point of contention like reprimanding a schoolboy trying to outrun discipline. Unfortunately I had long forgotten that I had just flipped over the table, which promptly tripped me from behind, bludgeoning my head on its edge. For a moment of dust-settling silence we lay there nearly expired, both afraid to move, neither one of us expecting the seemingly inanimate table to be the great leveler of the night. It was here, horizontal, where we continued our conversation.

"You alive, back there?" James asked, nervously annoyed. I immediately hocked a blood-streaked phlegm wad onto the wall beside us, somehow a "yes" and "fuck you" all rolled into one choking thrust of air. The sanguine slime stuck hard, staying dead above our heads with all the silence I could conjure. It was not my turn to talk.

"I realize we have past the point of no return, so you're gonna get every last detail as long as you fucking stay down and don't interrupt, vocally or physically! Understood!?!"

I spit again.

He took a deep breath and exhaled hard. "First off, this is *not* about me sleeping with her. That said, you are not going to be happy by the time I am done talking. If we can come to a mutual place of understanding, that something took place between two people, something that had nothing to do with you and…"

James interrupted himself, releasing a smothering mist of guilt, even further stiffening the dead air in the room.

"Okay." James said with a massive ulcerous breath, "So, I poured us both a scotch. By the time I turned around to face her she had already helped herself to the couch and laid down, nestling her own impression into the cushions. She had a comfortable grin on her face, which I remember thinking seemed a little over confident. I said something stupid, to the degree of 'Looks like you've made yourself comfortable' and she took it one step further, adding 'It feels more like a party than an appointment,' following with a large gulp of scotch, almost draining it in one sip."

I sighed heavily, "Yup, sounds like her!" briefly forgetting my vow of silence.

"You know how it goes with two people drinking sometimes. It's like an unconscious race. Anyway, she proceeded to talk, almost warning me about all the things she was about to spill, saying it was gonna take a lot of patience, understanding, some leaps of faith - same initial cautionary shit I hear from all my patients. But then she said I was too far away and that I needed to come closer. I was two fucking feet away from her, for Christsakes! So, I move closer, humoring her, and she goes into this breathy monologue how in order for a person like her to be as honest as possible, she needs to trust me further than what my profession may allow. Certain walls needed to come down, etc. She started rubbing my leg. I got nervous and excused myself, got us another couple drinks..."

"Oh! Nervous!!!" I half laughed, "More drinks!! Got it! Mooooooore drinks!" I threw my arms up, boiling over. Although it was clear any interrogation would be too late and irrelevant. I could tell this was leading somewhere far worse than an opportunist's hasty fuck. He was ignoring me, on a roll with his story.

"When I came back, she just continued on. Listen - SHE HAD ALREADY DECIDED SHE HAD TO FUCK ME TO, QUOTE UNQUOTE, FEEL CLOSER TO ME BEFORE SHE SPILLED HER GUTS!!! SHE SAID IT WAS A TRUST ISSUE!?!?"

"And..."

"AND I FUCKING INDULGED HER! RIGHT THEN AND THERE!!! DO YOU REALLY WANT THE GORY FUCKING DETAILS!?!"

"I do."

"HA! Well..." he paused and smiled, shaking his head, "...that means I'm gonna have to fast-forward a bit, buddy! The sex itself was fucking GREAT! Illicit! Spontaneous! Loud! Quick! Just how good sex SHOULD BE! Nothing gory there except a couple crusty white stains on a very EXPENSIVE leather couch!"

And with this, he sat up and glared down at me.

"Might I add, the trust level hit the fucking roof at that point!!!" He laughed himself dizzy while I stood up, now looking down at him in a world far beyond violence. Paralytic gut-steaming inertia had given me more vertigo than my blood alcohol. I leaned against the wall as he continued while his smile stayed put.

"So! We cleaned up and now it was time to *really* penetrate the situation! We talked the afternoon away in that great post-humpin' haze! She told me *all* about you. Everything. HA! Maybe THAT'S why I felt like I knew you from before!!!"

I hit him hard in the jaw with my right fist but before he fell he managed to grab my neck. His flailing weight pulled us down. He fell on top of me, quickly perching himself up into a rather homo-sexual straddle, before putting his knees into my arms, straight-jacketing me to the cold linoleum while he let out a burst of defiant guffaws in between words.

"And I am *SURE* you're dying to know what she said about you, huh? But really, think about it – what difference does it make? Why do *YOU* need to know everything *YOU* already *DID*? But I'll tell you one thing! Did you have *ANY* idea in the world she was three months pregnant when she saw me that day?"

And with this, he put his hands around my neck, applying just enough pressure to keep me in submission. Clearly it was not his hands that were causing my eyes to bulge the way they were at the moment. This choke was mere collateral, a pre-emptive attempt to make sure I didn't kill him before he finished his story. But we had reached a point beyond words, a point he was too blind to embrace,

as he continued to gab about the drinks they threw back, the co-
caine, the homespun Black Cohosh and grapefruit juice "remedy"
he made her drink, his midnight nervous breakdown causing him to
annihilate his fancy office as she miscarried in the bathroom. None
of this was of any consequence to me as *The Intrusion* had already
taken me over somewhere around the time he was pleading, that
because of this storm we mutually brewed, he and I might be cut
from the same cloth. As he made his closing statement of one of the
most bloody hole-ridden tales I hope I ever hear, I proved to him
the only way I knew how – in a grand finale of certain permanence
– that we were not the same.

ACKNOWLEDGMENTS

First and foremost to Jon and Tania of Traveling Shoes Press –
my brave high desert angels who swiftly rescued these books from
the mysterious fist of the industry, and again, to Jon for the masterful
design; to Jean-Paul Garnier, who continues to prove he is one step
ahead of me – this time with his final eagle-eye edits; to Joseph
Mattson, whose broad-stroke alterations (since withheld) would have
made it another great book in another place in another time, and to
the great Tav Falco, for the crackerjack foreword and sage encouragement. And to Travis Keats Ross, who seduced fate through his
good taste.

Special thanks also to the eyes that lent themselves to the early
shambolic versions of these stories: Alex Maslansky of Stories
Books, Lauren Everett, Hannah Blumenfeld, Zack Wentz, Barron
Graham Hart, John Tottenham, Gitane Demone (for art contribution
to the early incarnation), as well as Tyson for lessons learned and
time well spent.

Author and songwriter **Gabriel Hart** lives in Morongo Valley in California's High Desert. He was the man behind L.A. noir-punk band The Starvations, and presently he is leader of L.A. based punk Wall of Sound group Jail Weddings, who will release their third album *Blood Moon Blue* in 2019. Their previous album *Meltdown: A Declaration of Unpopular Emotion* (2013) was voted Best Album of The Year by *L.A. Weekly*, followed by Band of The Year in 2014.

Virgins In Reverse & The Intrusion is his debut novel (Traveling Shoes Press). His chapbooks *Cinema of Life* (2016) and *Nothing To See Here* (2017) will be incorporated into his upcoming speculative fiction novel *Lies of Heaven*, to be released in 2019. He is also presently immersed in *High Prey Drive*, his teenage initiation novel project.

His short stories and poetry have been published in *Cholla Needles*, the *Desert Writers Guild Anthology*, *Luna Arcana* as well as Space Cowboy's *Simultaneous Times* anthology and podcast. He is also a regular contributor to *L.A. Record*, a Los Angeles underground music publication.

Gabrielhart.net

OTHER BOOKS FROM TRAVELING SHOES PRESS

Emmy Albertina Bogaerts

Emmy, The Memoir of a Flemish Immigrant

Jon Christopher

Somewhere Out There In The West
Moving At The Speed Of Time
Meanwhile There Were Dragons
Realistic Hallucinations

Jean-Paul L. Garnier

Echo of Creation

Mark Leysen

The Klown

Nora Novak

Los Feliz Confidential, A Memoir

TRAVELINGSHOESPRESS.COM